I0760883

LOVE BEYOND MAGIC

BOOK 13 OF MORNA'S LEGACY SERIES

BETHANY CLAIRE

Copyright 2022 by Bethany Claire
All rights reserved.

License Notes

All rights reserved. This book or any portion thereof may not be reproduced or used in any manner whatsoever without the express written permission of the author except for the use of brief quotations in a book review.

This story is a work of fiction. Names, characters, places, and incidents are either products of the author's imagination or used fictitiously. Any resemblance to actual events, locales, or persons, living or dead, is entirely coincidental.

Cover Designed by Damonza

Available In eBook, Paperback, & Hardback
eBook ISBN: 978-1-970110-61-6
Paperback ISBN: 978-1-970110-70-8
Hardback ISBN: 978-1-970110-71-5

For Vivian Sullivan Nwankpah,
A dedicated reader and a loyal friend.
You were such a big part of Bethany's Book Babes,
and you helped me so much throughout the years.
Thank you.
You will be so very missed.

CHAPTER 1

Seattle, WA
Present Day

Peter lay panting next to me as I rolled over on my side toward him, my eyes brimming with tears. I found it difficult to put my finger on why this time felt so different from all the times before. Why this time at the conclusion of our weirdly regimented—every Friday at ten p.m. —lovemaking session, I just knew that I could never do it again.

One might assume it was the fact that after eight years together, I was tired of waiting on an engagement, but deep down I knew that really wasn't it. I could always propose, and I knew Peter would say yes. In truth, I really lived much more in fear that someday he would ask me to marry him rather than disappointment that he hadn't yet.

It could be the realization of just how bad the sex was, but it's not like that was a new revelation either. He always seemed to enjoy himself. It wasn't even that Peter was an especially selfish lover. It was only that about three years in, I grew so tired of coaching him towards exactly what felt good to me with no real success, that I eventually just gave in and became adept at faking it. It seemed that no matter what we did, what we tried, from my side of things we just weren't clicking the way I thought two people in love should.

In my defense, I really was flying blind in terms of examples of what a real romantic relationship should be. My sister, Rory, and I grew up with two of the most platonic married people we, or any of our childhood friends, ever knew. They had separate bedrooms, separate schedules, separate interests. But they both loved us, and no one could deny the intense friendship they shared. For them, that had always seemed to be enough.

For me though, I could no longer deny that life spent with a great friend would never be anywhere close to enough—even if that friend was as good, and kind, and enjoyable to be around as Peter. That was really the crux of it, I think. I knew that my life needed to be filled with more: more passion, more laughter, more risk, more of just about everything other than whatever this was that I was doing with the sweet guy lying beside me.

I'd not planned any of it. Not what I would say, or even that I was going to say it. But as tears began to roll down my face, I reached out and touched his shoulder.

"Peter?"

"Yeah?" He exhaled, a happy grin on his face as he clasped his hands over his stomach and closed his eyes. My lips trembled as the true measure of pain I was about to cause him set in. He didn't want any more than what we had. He was as content as he'd ever felt a need to be. And I was completely sure that he would never understand why I was not.

"Did he cry or scream at you? Did he do anything?"

In the end, my worry over Peter had turned out to be just another symptom of how much more I seemed to feel than those around me. The thought of hurting him hurt me far more than it had actually pained him.

I shook my head as Rory and I carefully lowered the three-tier wedding cake into the back of our delivery van.

"No. He was stone. He nodded. Said he understood, and that he would begin moving his stuff out today. Then he rolled over and went to sleep."

"Ugh." Rory grimaced as we closed the back doors and waved off our driver. "I always liked Peter well enough, but that's slightly scary that his reaction would be so, well, reactionless."

I shrugged. "I think it's just evidence of where we really were. I don't feel too devastated about it either. Looking back, I can't even begin to remember why I was ever drawn to him."

"I know exactly why. He's familiar. He's so much like Mom and Dad."

She was right. But I wasn't like either one of them. Neither was Rory.

"Are you sure they're our actual parents?"

Rory laughed. "Honestly, no. But I mean, I'm pretty sure. We both have Mom's nose."

Once back inside our bakery, Rory moved to lock the front door and switch off the open sign while I began cleaning up for the day. We worked quietly together for a few minutes before Rory spoke again, her voice soft and hesitant when she did.

"Can I be honest with you, Olivia?"

"Of course."

"I sort of want to break up, too."

My hand stopped dragging the wet, soapy rag over our countertop.

"Have you been seeing someone? Why didn't you tell me?"

"No. I mean, I wish, but no. I want to break up with this job. With this place. We're both not happy here, Liv. I feel like this business is about as emotionless for us as you and Peter's relationship. This was Dad's baby, not ours. Let's sell it."

Selling the bakery had never crossed my mind. It didn't seem like an option. When Dad retired and handed the business down to us, we both felt like it was our responsibility to keep it going.

"Would it break Dad's heart?"

"Maybe. But we're breaking our own hearts by settling here. Let's sell it, then take some of the profit and take a big, long trip while we try to figure out what is next for each of us."

Change must've been in the air because for the second time in as many days, my next move seemed clear.

"Okay, I'm down. Where do we want to go?"

The empty fishbowl sat in front of us filled with a small piece of paper for each and every country that would be even remotely safe for us to travel to. I desperately wanted to go to New Zealand. Rory wanted to go to Spain.

After hours of arguing, we finally decided to leave the decision up to fate.

We flipped a coin to see who would draw. Rory won.

Closing her eyes, she reached deep inside, swirling the pieces of paper around until she was satisfied that everything was mixed up enough for her to finally make her pick.

She pulled out her choice, opened it up, and we both looked down at our fate: Scotland.

We both groaned in disappointment.

"It rains so much in Scotland. Don't we get enough of that here in Seattle? Let's just try again, right?"

Rory nodded, tossing Scotland back into the bunch and enthusiastically shaking up the bowl. "You pick this time."

I did as she asked and pulled out Scotland.

We tried again and pulled Scotland out once more.

After the fourth try, we both surrendered to the possibility that maybe something akin to fate was at play.

"Well, I guess we are going to Scotland, huh, Liv?"

I reached for my laptop to reluctantly begin research for the one destination where we were just as likely to need a raincoat as we did at home.

CHAPTER 2

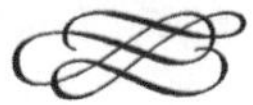

Buchannan Castle
Isle of Skye, Scotland
17th Century

Shaky hands rested upon the handle of the large, carved wooden doors that towered above him as he stood outside his childhood home. He'd finally run as far as his feet would take him, and somehow he'd ended up where everything had begun.

For months, Paton roamed every mile of Scotland away from the Isle of Eight Lairds, searching for a way to heal his grief. Nothing worked. No new place, nor work, not even all the women he'd taken to bed in search of distraction helped to ease the pain and guilt that pulsed through him with every beat of his heart.

Only time would cause the memories to fade.

"Are ye well, me Lord? I've ne'er seen ye look quite so pale."

Paton dropped his hands to his side and turned to look at his loyal companion.

"How many times do I have to tell ye, Davy? Doona call me, 'me Lord.' I worked right alongside ye for months. I canna be but a handful of years older than ye."

His friend shrugged. "Aye, I know ye did, but ye had somewhere to go once Old Man Henry had no more use of our services, and I dinna, yet ye allowed me to come with ye, so ye are me master now, and I shall call ye 'my Lord,' as long as I am under yer employ."

Paton sighed, relenting. There were far bigger worries on his mind. During his months away, he'd done his best to gather information about the state of his home, and the news that had come to him only added to his grief.

Both of his parents had passed away in the last year. While he'd never known her, his brother had lost his betrothed, as well. The castle of his childhood—once brimming with activity, joy, and laughter—was no more.

Paton still couldn't believe he'd gotten this close to the castle unseen. The grounds should've been brimming with servants in the gardens or near the stables. Today, during his approach, all he found was stillness.

While Paton had known that his leaving with Nicol as a young lad would someday mean his younger brother, Bram, would eventually become Laird, he'd never dreamed it would happen so soon. How was Bram coping with the responsibility on his own? And what of his sister? She'd been just a bairn when he left. She wouldn't know him. Would she accept his presence here after all this time? For that matter, would Bram?

Questions and worry swirled in his mind as he continued to stare hesitantly at the doorway.

"Ye dinna answer, me Lord. Do ye need to sit a moment?"

Paton pushed the exhausting thoughts away to answer Davy. "Nae, I'm fine. 'Tis only I doona think I should enter uninvited. They will think me a stranger. None within the castle will recognize me."

Davy's brows pulled together doubtfully. "Have ye truly changed so much?"

Paton could scarcely recognize his own reflection after his years with the faeries. Gone was his youthful complexion and boyish frame. He stood six inches taller, his muscles were now sculpted and strong, his voice was a full octave deeper, and his skin was now darkened by the months spent in the sun.

Perhaps some of him still looked the same. He assumed he still had the same nose, maybe the same smile, but all else was changed. Even his long hair was now cropped shorter than most men he knew.

"Aye. More than ye would ever understand. I was a boy when I was taken from here."

Swallowing to gather his courage, Paton lifted his hand to knock.

Time dragged as they waited. Just as Paton lifted his fist to knock once more, the doors began to creak open.

Chambers, his father's oldest confidant and servant, who'd been old when he was a child and now looked ancient, appeared in the cracked opening. It was the first familiar face he'd seen in years. Paton's eyes rebelliously filled with tears at the sight of him.

"Aye? May I help ye? 'Tis late for the laird to receive visitors."

"Chambers, I know that I doona look as I once did, but 'tis me, Paton."

The old man's eyebrows lifted before he squinted and leaned in closer through the doorway opening. He stared at him silently for a moment before pushing open the door and stepping forward shakily with his arms wide open.

"Och, Paton. When ye dinna come home after either of yer parents died, we were all certain we'd ne'er see ye again."

Paton gripped the old man tightly as unrelenting tears began to freely flow.

"I only learned of their deaths. Had I known and had I been able, I would've come."

"O'course, lad. I ne'er doubted that. Ye must come inside. Please tell me that ye can stay awhile. Ye canna know how much Bram needs ye."

"I am here for good, Chambers."

"Chambers, who is here?"

A young female voice echoed through the entryway. As Paton stepped inside, he looked up to find a woman who could only possibly be his sister.

"Christ, lass. Ye look just like mother."

Ella's face wrinkled in confusion as she walked toward them.

"'Tis yer eldest brother, me Lady."

Ella's eyes locked suspiciously with his own before she quickly turned her back toward him to call out for their brother.

"Bram!"

"I doona mean to unsettle ye, lass. I know that I was not expected."

She turned back toward him, her voice sure and steady.

"Ye doona unsettle me. 'Tis only that I doona know ye, and Bram does. He will wish to see ye, aye? Ye should be warned that Bram isna himself this evening. He is rarely himself, as of late."

"What do ye…" His question was interrupted by the arrival of his younger brother, who staggered into the entryway on unsteady feet.

"What is it, lass?" Bram's words slurred as he neared them.

"It seems our brother has returned home."

Bram's head whipped toward him as they began to look each other over.

"Ye must be mistaken, Ella. Paton is dead to this family. He abandoned us years ago. I doona know, nor do I care, who this man is."

Without another word, Bram turned from him and left the room, the coolness of his words reverberating through Paton's body.

"Ella, lass, I am yer brother despite what Bram has said."

She nodded, her eyes sad and weary. "Aye, I know. He knows that, too." She paused long enough to direct her attention to Chambers. "Please have a room readied for Paton, Chambers. Mayhap in the morn, Bram will be of a clearer mind to handle all of this."

In much the same way as his brother, Ella turned to leave, making the entryway feel cool and empty. Paton's heart grew heavy as Chambers began to see him and Davy further into the castle.

"Doona fash, lad. Grief has made him angry with ye, but his love for ye willna allow him to hold on to it for long. Welcome home. It does this old man's heart good to see another

Buchannan back under this roof. Yer parents would be so glad to see ye back here."

Paton nodded obligingly, although he truly suspected that their own welcome would've been much like Bram's. Even so, he made one silent promise to himself as he followed Chambers through the familiar hallways of the castle: He would see to it that Bram and Ella were cared for. With everyone else now gone, he would give all he had left to the only two people he still loved in the world.

CHAPTER 3

Seattle, WA

Six Months Later - Present Day

Tick. Tick. Tick.

"Now!"

Rory screamed as the second hand finally shifted the clock over to five. At the sound of her command, I threw our cake shop 'open' sign to 'closed,' and locked the door before facing her as we squealed in unison.

Our last day of work was finally here. In a matter of minutes, we would be passing on the bakery keys to the new owners and setting off on our Scottish adventure.

"Are we sure everything is ready to go?"

I already knew that it was. While we'd found buyers fairly quickly, they'd wanted us to stay on for a few months to help make the transition easier. We'd agreed, and a few months had somehow turned into six. By this point, we were really more staff to the new owners than anything else. To let us say our goodbyes, they'd left our last day at the shop to us to run alone.

Rory smiled, the keys to the shop dangling on one finger.

"Yes. It's finally time to say goodbye to this place."

I nodded, as an unexpected sadness filled my chest.

"Ya know, I really thought Dad would come by today to say goodbye to this place."

Rory shrugged. She was always much better at keeping things from bothering her than I was.

"He's still angry. It's fine. He'll get over it. I'd rather him be disappointed in me than for me to make it to eighty and be disappointed in myself for all of the things I didn't do out of obligation to him."

While logically I agreed with her, I couldn't shake the guilt I felt at ending the business that our father had worked so hard to build. Even though we'd been running it on our own for years, it had always still felt like his.

Rory stepped in front of my line of vision and gripped my shoulders before leaning her forehead in close to mine. "Your thoughts are basically screaming at me. Let me emphasize this again, Liv: this is *our* bakery now. Dad gave it up when we took over. It's ours to do with it what we please, including selling it. It's fine. Let's just enjoy this."

I breathed deeply and shook out my shoulders to loosen myself up as I took one last glance around the shop. "You're right. It's done. And it's time. Let's get out of here. Scotland awaits."

. . .

Somewhere Outside of Edinburgh, Scotland
One Day Later

The roundabout sped closer as we climbed our way up the hill. Jet-lagged, lost, and driving a vehicle I honestly had no business driving, my anxiety grew with each passing minute.

"Rory, which exit do I take?"

I glanced out of the corner of my eye to see her frantically fiddling with the map we'd picked up at a gas station on the outskirts of Edinburgh.

"Umm…I'm thinking the second one?"

I pushed the blinker toward left, as I gripped the steering wheel tightly with my right hand and reached for the gear shift with my left.

"You're *thinking* the second?"

She scrunched up her nose nervously as she answered me. "Yeah…I mean, I think so. You should look at this map, Olivia. There are so many tiny roads. I'm having a really hard time navigating it."

"Okay, the second exit it is." I cautiously entered the roundabout, shifted gears in a way that lurched the car jerkily forward, and with absolutely no confidence, took the left exit that sent us barreling onto a one-lane road. Since leaving Edinburgh, we'd stayed on larger, multi-lane roads, but now, I'd just steered us onto a road so narrow I found it difficult to believe it was actually meant to be driven on by modern-day vehicles.

"What am I supposed to do when we meet up with another car? This road is barely big enough for us."

Rory leaned forward in her seat in what I could only assume was an attempt to see further into the distance. "Is this entire damned country on a curve?"

I nodded, as I gripped the wheel more tightly. "It does seem that way. Look." I nodded ahead of us. "There's a road marker. Are we going in the right direction?"

A few seconds ticked by as Rory wrestled with the map once more. "Yes! Thank God. It doesn't look like we are all that far now. I think you'll just follow this road until the next intersection where you'll turn right. Then the hotel should just be straight down that next road."

"Great. Now, I just need to figure out what to do now." I gestured ahead of us to where a car came speeding toward us.

On instinct, I shifted downward and slowed down, only relaxing when I noticed the approaching vehicle pull off into the smallest of round shoulders on the left side of the road.

"So, whoever reaches a pull-off first, pulls over so the other person can pass?" Rory asked the question as I hesitantly sped by the now-stopped vehicle.

"I guess so." I exhaled shakily as my breathing began to return to normal. "Tomorrow before we leave the hotel, I think we should ask the front desk if there's another car rental close. I'm a nervous wreck driving this thing. I don't think I can do it for the next month."

Nothing was safe about our current travel situation. Not only had we both been up for well past twenty-four hours, but this was only my second time to ever drive a manual transmission vehicle, and I was doing so while driving on the other side of the car, on the other side of the road.

"I agree. I can't believe the rental place gave up the automatic car we'd reserved just because we were a few hours late. It's not like we could do anything about the flight delay. Are you okay? Do you want me to drive?"

I chuckled and shook my head. Rory's driving scared me back home. There was no way I was letting her drive us around here.

"I'm alright. Like you said, we're close."

"Yeah, we are! Look! I think that's Loch Lomond."

As we rounded yet another endless curve, the road ahead of us opened up to some of the most beautiful landscape I'd ever seen. As I stared ahead at the water, the rolling hills, and our castle-like hotel in the distance, all of my jet lag and frustration over our vehicle melted away.

"I have a good feeling about this trip, Rory. I think Scotland might be just where we were supposed to travel to, after all."

CHAPTER 4

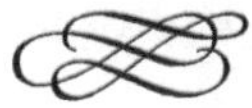

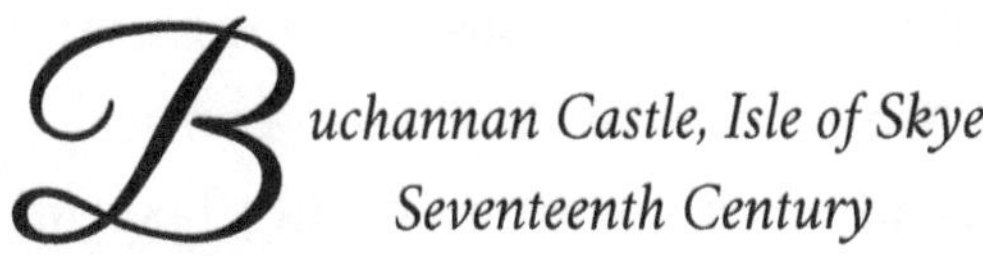

Buchannan Castle, Isle of Skye
Seventeenth Century

"Are ye quite certain 'tis no' rotten, Davy? It neither looks nor smells appetizing."

Paton didn't mean to dash his spirit. He knew he was only trying to help, but he truly didn't know if he could get himself to eat a single bite of the mystery meat that lay in front of him.

"Aye, I am. I butchered the animal meself only this afternoon. I've already eaten some, and I feel fine for it. Mayhap it willna taste as bad to ye as it looks."

Paton raised his left brow as he cast a glance over at the other side of the table where both Bram and Ella sat staring down at their plate with dread. Neither seemed eager to test Davy's dish.

The expressions on the faces of their guests on the other side of the table were even worse.

"And what was yer own opinion when ye tasted it? Did ye enjoy it?"

Davy ducked his head and sighed. "Nae me Lord. 'Tis rubbish, but I give ye me word that it willna make ye ill. Though, in truth I doona know what ye expected. I've ne'er claimed to be a cook."

Paton sighed and pushed the food away before standing to pat Davy on the shoulder. "Aye, I know. There was no reason for me to expect ye to know how to cook. 'Tis only our most urgent need now that Gawen has run off so unexpectedly. I thought we would see if ye were suited for it."

Dismissing Davy, Paton returned to his seat to address their unexpected guests—Laird Morton and his eldest son Lanrick.

"I apologize for the state of our dinner this evening. It seems our cook has gone missing."

"'Tis no concern. In truth, I dinna come here to dine. There is a reason for our visit today, but mayhap the young lass should excuse herself before we begin our discussion."

Paton frowned and held out his hand to gesture for his sister to stay. Everything about Laird Morton made him uneasy. The man's pores seemed to ooze malice.

"The lass will remain at the table, Thayne. She isna a child. She can hear whate'er business ye need to discuss."

Laird Morton's eyes flashed angrily, and Paton watched as the old man worked to compose himself before speaking again.

"She is a woman, Paton. If ye think it right for her to be here, what other wrongful customs did ye pick up during all the years ye spent away?"

"I expect a great many."

Laird Morton's throat made a gruff, growling sound as his jaw tightened. "Ye've certainly taken over the role of laird here quickly, lad. In truth, I thought 'twould be Bram I would be speaking to. Even when the two of ye were young, he was the more agreeable of the two of ye. What has he done to deserve ye stealing what rightfully became his after ye abandoned yer family?"

Before Paton could answer, Bram spoke up beside him.

"Paton has done nothing, Laird Morton. I ne'er wanted to own this land, nor oversee it. I have happily signed ownership of the land back over to me brother."

"Only a fool wouldna wish to own this land."

Paton stood, his body tense with anger. "Thayne, I willna have ye insult the members of this household while ye are under our roof. Either tell us the reason for yer visit or leave."

Laird Morton laughed insincerely, before looking toward his son and extending his hand as Lanrick reached to his side and pulled out a scroll before handing it off to his father.

"I dinna mean to insult ye. Here is the reason for me visit. I dinna wish to trouble Bram with this so soon after yer father's death, but I believe more than enough time has passed now, and I've no desire for this to be put off any longer." Pausing, Laird Morton pulled the scroll straight with his bony fingers in front of Paton, taking care to point to the seal of their father's signet ring that signed the bottom of the page.

Paton read over the scroll quickly, his heart sinking as his eyes traveled over the document.

"I doona believe our father would have agreed to any such arrangement."

Once again, Laird Morton pointed to the seal. "Is that no' yer father's?"

"Aye, 'tis, but he would ne'er have agreed to this."

"Paton." Pain filled Bram's voice as he spoke beside him. "Many years ago, I know that Da struggled with a shortage of tenants and bad crops. I dinna know of this arrangement, but I do know that he grew rather desperate for a verra long time."

Paton tore his furious gaze away from Laird Morton long enough to look at his brother. Sliding the parchment toward him, Paton pointed to the piece of the agreement no part of him could believe.

"So ye believe he would do this, then?"

It took only seconds for Bram's cheeks to flush as he pushed himself away from the table.

"Nae. Da wouldna have done this."

Laird Morton persisted. "I doona know what to tell ye lads. 'Tis yer father's signet. I've no other proof, nor do I require any."

Bram protested once more. "I can mayhap believe that Da asked ye for money, but he would never have willingly involved Ella in any of this."

"He what?" Ella's voice cracked as her voice rose in panic. "What could I possibly have to do with any of this?"

Laird Morton smiled. "I've wished for our families to be joined together for decades, but yer father always resisted me proposals. When he was in dire need, I was eager to help, but made certain that if his luck dinna turn around, then I would finally get something I wanted. I loaned yer father a great deal of money, lass, and he failed to pay back what was owed in time. Ye are now betrothed to me son."

Paton watched as Bram reached for their sister's hand, but she snatched it away as she, too, rose from her seat.

"I will do no such thing. I doona care what that piece of parchment says. I am too young."

Paton pushed the document away as he struggled to remain calm. "Ye must see that she is right, Thayne. The lass is only fourteen. While Lanrick must be at least thirty. Ye canna expect me to go along with this. How much is still owed?"

"Most are married at such an age, as ye well know. And half of the balance is unpaid. Payments ceased shortly after yer mother's death."

Paton looked down at the document again, taking care to read all of its stipulations. "The balance came due after our father's death, and we dinna know of the debt. Ye canna hold our family to this when we had no chance to pay it."

"Well…" Laird Morton paused as a devilish grin spread across his face. "Do ye have the funds to see this settled then?"

They didn't. Nowhere close. But Paton would figure out something. There was no other choice.

"Our father's debt came due three months after his death. The only decent thing to do is give us that much time to acquire the funds. If I am unable to pay the note in full at the end of three months, we will keep the arrangement, and yer son may marry Ella."

With a scream, Ella ran from the room as Laird Morton smiled.

"'Tis a large sum, lad, and rumors of yer penchant for allowing tenants to pay no rent without consequence from either of ye make it hard for me to believe ye will be able to find such an amount before then."

Paton shrugged, dread settling into a familiar place inside him. There was only one way to find such a sum so quickly, and it was the last thing on earth he wanted to do.

"Either way, ye shall still receive something ye want, Laird Morton. Do ye agree?"

The old man extended his bony fingers toward Paton. "Fine. Ye have three months. Not one day more. Good luck, Laird Buchannan. I believe ye shall need it."

CHAPTER 5

Loch Lomond, Scotland
Present Day

"Don't do it, Rory. I promise you'll regret it."

Ignoring me, she kicked off her shoes, threw her arms up over her head, stretched as she yawned, and then yanked back the covers on her bed and crawled inside.

"And I promise you, that I won't. I'm exhausted. And I'm a better sleeper than you. I pretty much guarantee that if I go to sleep right now, I'll be able to sleep until morning."

I glared at her, more jealous than upset. "It's only 6 p.m."

She smiled at me as she snuggled deeper into the bed. "I know. That means I'll get at least a whole twelve hours and wake up totally adjusted to the time change. I'll be rested and ready to go."

I frowned and reached for my coat before muttering the words, *'lucky bitch'* under my breath on my way out of our hotel room.

Rory was right. I wasn't nearly as good of a sleeper as she was. Even though my limbs were shaky from jet lag and my brain screamed at me to sleep, I knew if I did, I would be awake at midnight and my circadian rhythm would be ruined for a few days more.

I had to stay up until at least ten, which meant I had to find some way to entertain myself for the next few hours.

I was too tired to be hungry, but seeing as our hotel wasn't close to anything else, I figured my best bet to pass some time was to try to get a table at the hotel restaurant. As I approached to see only one table in the small round room occupied, I knew it wouldn't be a problem.

After approaching the host, I was quickly ushered to a two-person table directly next to the restaurant's other diners. It felt strange that they wouldn't have spaced us out to give the couple more privacy, but I said nothing as the man pulled out my chair and placed a menu in front of me.

"We serve simple, native food, lass. We source everything that we can from local farmers, and the rest we get from organic, sustainable sources. If ye are a guest of the hotel, everything will be billed to yer room. Someone will be along shortly to take yer order. I hope ye enjoy yer meal."

With a curt nod, the man left, and I hesitantly began to look over the menu as I tried to ignore the stares of the couple next to me. After only a few seconds, the woman spoke.

"I would recommend the soup if ye want something light. Jerry got the fish supper, and he enjoyed it."

I lifted my head and looked over at the woman to offer a

smile. "Thank you. I appreciate the recommendation. I didn't mean to intrude on your evening. I don't know why they sat me so close to you when there are plenty of other empty tables."

The old woman waved a dismissive hand. "Nonsense, lass. I, for one, enjoy company, and I'm sure Jerry is glad for it, too, for it means he will have to talk less if I have someone else to talk to. That is, if ye are the talking sort. If ye wish to eat yer meal in peace, I o'course understand that, as well."

"Oh, I'm a talker, too. Feel free to talk away. I'm trying to keep myself awake for a few hours anyway, so I welcome the conversation. My sister and I only arrived today, and we are more than a little jet lagged. She's already given up and gone to bed."

For the first time, the old man, Jerry, spoke. "I canna say that I blame her. 'Tis a long journey from the States. Where abouts are ye from?"

"Seattle. What about you two? Are you from the area?"

The woman—I still didn't know her name—answered. "We are a few hours out on the other side of Edinburgh, so no, we doona live close to here. We just wanted to get away for a long weekend together"

"Well, I haven't had the chance to see much of it yet, but it seems like a beautiful place to do just that."

"Aye, 'tis." She paused and nodded toward the waiter so I would turn to look at him as he approached. "Does anything strike yer fancy, lass?"

I nodded and ordered the soup per the old woman's suggestion. When the waiter left, I turned back toward the friendly old woman. "I'm sorry. I don't think I ever caught your name. I'm Olivia, Liv, for short."

The woman nodded almost as if she already knew that,

although I didn't remember introducing myself earlier. "My name is Morna, dear. Now tell me more about this trip ye and yer sister are on. Where are ye headed next?"

"I believe we are headed to the Isle of Mull next. We are supposed to catch the ferry tomorrow afternoon."

Morna shook her head and clucked her tongue at me, regretfully. "I'm afraid ye will have to change yer plans, lass. All ferries to and from Mull have been suspended until further notice. Last I heard, they thought it would be weeks before they were running again."

My eyes widened in surprise. I'd received a confirmation email from the inn we were set to check in to only this morning.

"Really? Wouldn't the hotel have notified me if I wasn't going to be able to make it over there?"

Morna shrugged. "Aye, ye would assume so, but I can assure ye, that ye willna be getting to the isle. All the ferry operators have gone on strike. Where are ye supposed to go after Mull?"

"Um..." I racked my brain for the mental itinerary I should've known by heart for as many times as I'd gone over it with Rory. "I think after Mull we were headed to the Isle of Skye, but our reservation there isn't for another four nights."

"Best ye call them in the morning and see if ye can check-in early. Likely, if they doona have room for ye, they will suggest somewhere else on the isle ye can stay."

Morna must have taken in the exasperated expression on my face for it didn't take long for her to continue.

"Doona fash though, lass. There is much to see on Skye, even if ye just spend a day or two driving around and taking in the beauty of it. Ye must drive through the Quiraing. 'Tis a splendor to behold, I assure ye. And do promise that ye will take yer time when doing so. Stop when feel like it, wander around. If ye do get lost, ye'll find yer way back eventually."

I smiled as the waiter approached with a bowl of steaming hot soup extended out in front of him. "I don't know about that. We had a hard enough time making our way here. If we just let ourselves explore without some sort of map, I'm not sure we will find our way back."

She dismissed me with a wave of her hand. "Nonsense, 'tis part of the joy of travel."

She stood suddenly, bringing the conversation to an abrupt end.

"I can tell by the look in Jerry's eye, he's long past ready for bed. Best we be off for the night. 'Twas lovely to meet ye, lass. I hope ye enjoy every minute of yer time in Scotland. And doona forget what I said about Skye. Allow yerself to explore it a bit. Ye've no excuse not to now that ye have several extra days ye dinna plan on having there."

Jerry gave me a polite nod and a smile, and with that, the old couple left me alone to my soup. It was delicious, but I couldn't enjoy it. All I could think about was how nothing seemed to be going according to plan on the trip we'd spent months meticulously planning. First, the rental car. Now, we would have to reroute an entire portion of the trip. The whole thing made me uneasy.

I shook my head to push the feeling away. There was no reason for me to feel uneasy. While, admittedly, I'd not done much of it, I supposed every trip was met with a few challenges. My overreaction to all of it was simply due to exhaustion—everything just felt more stressful than it otherwise would.

The rest of the trip would progress just splendidly.

I just knew it.

CHAPTER 6

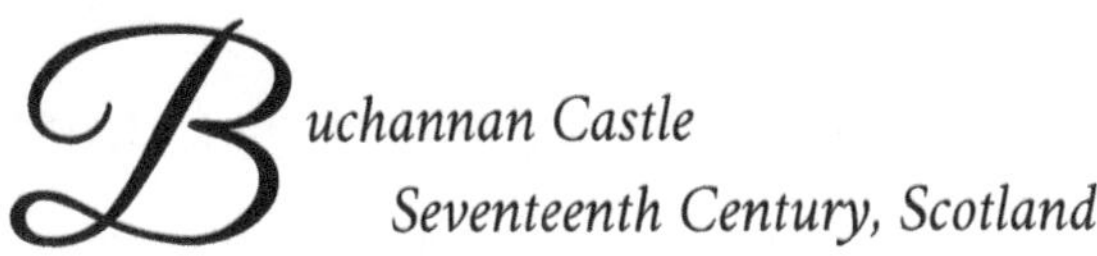

Buchannan Castle
Seventeenth Century, Scotland

Paton knocked on his sister's bedchamber door for the third time in the span of a few hours. Still she refused to answer him.

"Lass, ye must let me in. I truly doona wish to break down the door, but if ye doona at least answer me so I know ye are still within the walls of this castle, I shall."

For the first time all morning, the sound of his sister groaning traveled through the closed door. A moment later, he could hear her footsteps approaching.

The handle jiggled before she cracked the door open enough to peer out at him, her eyes red and puffy from tears.

"Ye've betrayed me, brother. I know that ye dinna grow up

with me, but I still canna believe ye would betray me so. Ye canna allow me to marry that vile man."

"If ye would permit me to enter, I will explain."

The door flung open as Ella stepped to the side, permitting him entry.

"There is nothing ye may say that will make this right, brother."

"Lass, I needed that man to remove himself from our home so I said what would get him to leave with the most haste. But I promise ye this, I willna allow ye to marry Lanrick."

His sister eyed him skeptically. "I'm no fool, Paton. I know we doona have the funds to pay Da's debts."

Paton sighed. "Aye, I know, but I believe I know where we may be able to get the money we need. It seems I must find myself a wife whose father's wealth outmatches Laird Morton's."

"In three months?" Ella's expression remained hopeless as she crossed her arms and moved to sit on the edge of her bed. "Ye've been gone for so long, Paton. Ye doona know anyone here. Ye've no relationships with other lairds. How will ye find one who wishes to marry their daughter off to ye. And what of her? Do ye truly expect to find one who wishes to marry ye in such a short amount of time? Most lassies I know would prefer to know the man they marry."

"They may prefer it, but ye must know that 'tis rarely a luxury women are afforded."

"And ye think that is right?"

He'd only known the girl six months, yet he loved her completely. His sister's fiery spirit reminded him of his own when he was younger.

"I dinna say that. I only meant that no lass will be surprised if their father makes the arrangement without them—before they've gotten a chance to know me. O'course I would prefer it if I can find someone I would truly wish to wed, but with the funds we require, my options will be limited. I'll be happy to settle for someone who doesna drive me mad."

Ella stood as Chambers appeared in the doorway.

"There is someone here from the village that wishes to see ye, Paton."

Paton turned to face the old man. "Who is it?"

"Miren."

Miren.

Paton's breath came short at the sound of her name. What would the lass look like after all these years? Still lovely, to be sure. But, what of him? He knew just how different he looked now—what time and his years with the faeries had done to him. She'd loved him as a boy. She'd never known him as a man.

"She's married now." Bram suddenly appeared in the doorway next to Chambers. "I thought ye should know before ye went down to see her. How Murray Black convinced that sweet lass to marry him I will never understand. He is perhaps the vilest man on this half of the isle."

Of course Miren was married by now. Paton wouldn't expect different of a lass as lovely as she, but it pained him to know that her spouse wasn't worthy of her. If fate had treated them differently, if the onset of his since-destroyed powers hadn't caused him to leave his home when he was just becoming a man, Miren would've been his bride. No part of him doubted it.

He quickly redirected his attention back to Ella. "Whatever I have to do, lass, ye may rest easy knowing that ye willna wed Lanrick Morton."

Brushing his way between Chambers and his brother, Paton hurried through the castle halls to see his childhood love for the first time since returning home. He smiled brightly as he stepped into the castle's entryway but stopped short at the sight of the woman awaiting him.

The lass looked nothing like the image he held of her in his mind. It was Miren, to be sure, but she seemed smaller, her shoulders slumped over as if to hide herself, and her entire frame seemed tight in a way that made it appear as if she perpetually held her breath. And something about the way she looked at him as their eyes locked made his chest hurt.

"I already told the lad before. I need to speak with the laird. No one else will do."

At least she hadn't lost the ability to speak up for herself.

"Aye, I know what ye told him, Miren. I am the laird."

Miren gave one shake of her head, before continuing.

"Nae, ye are no more laird than I am. I've known the Buchannan's me entire life. Doona ye think I would know what Paton looks like. I need to speak with him this instant. Me husband will be needing me back home shortly. He is verra badly injured, and I've no arrangement made for anyone else to care for him while I am away. I was only able to leave because the sleeping dram I'd given him had just begun to take effect."

She doesn't know. She doesn't recognize me. The thought coursed through Paton's mind as he continued to look Miren over. He'd suspected his appearance would come as a shock to her, but the realization that she found him to be a stranger wounded him.

"Miren, lass. Do ye truly no' know me?"

Miren took one unsteady step toward him, her eyes squinting as her face grew pale.

"Paton? I…I am sorry. Ye doona look the same."

Paton frowned uncomfortably. "Aye, lass, I know."

Paton barely had time to open his arms as Miren's expression relaxed and she propelled herself toward him, wrapping her arms around him in the tightest embrace he could remember.

Even Chamber's embrace hadn't been so tight.

"I doona think I realized just how much I'd missed ye until just now, Paton. Are ye well?"

"Well enough, lass."

Afraid she might ask him more questions, Paton tried to direct the conversation back to the reason for her visit.

"Ye said before that yer husband is injured. Is that why ye've come? Do ye need help?"

"Nae." She hesitated. "I mean, aye. Aye, I do need help, but no' in the way I'm sure ye would expect. I want work, Paton. Me husband's leg was shattered by his horse. He canna work. He willna be able to work for some time. In truth, I doona know if he will ever be the same again. And we must pay rent and keep food on the table."

"Ye needn't worry about yer rent until yer husband is well. Surely ye know that I wouldna evict ye."

Miren shook her head firmly. "Nae, Paton. We will pay what we owe, as we always have. I just need the means to do so."

He could understand that.

"Can ye cook, lass?" He asked the question with more enthusiasm than he intended, but with two meals past since their chef abandoned him, his stomach growled hungrily.

"Aye, o'course I can."

"I shall pay ye well to do that, if ye are willing."

Miren smiled, and he thought he saw her straighten up, just a bit.

"Aye. I would love to. May I begin tomorrow?"

Paton nodded. "Aye. I shall bring a horse and cart down into the village tomorrow so we can load it with supplies for the kitchen. Then I'll see ye back here."

"Thank ye. If ye doona have any objection, I shall stop off and place an order for a fortnight's worth of supplies when I return to the village. It should be ready by mid-morning. We could meet at Seamus' cabin at midday. I know ye intend for me to start most days earlier, but the morrow might be difficult without proper provisions."

"That sounds perfect, lass. I doona think any of us shall starve." His stomach growled as if it doubted him.

Miren gave him a nod and turned to leave before twisting her head to speak to him once more.

"Paton, I meant to ask ye earlier, why are ye back now? Did the old laird finally let all of ye go?"

Paton's teeth clenched together. He'd not spoken a word of anything that had happened since his return.

"In a way. He's dead, lass. All who lived on the Isle of Eight Lairds are dead."

Miren's face paled, but she said nothing else as she turned her back to him and left, leaving him gripped by the grief he felt each time the lifeless bodies of all those he'd so loved on the isle flashed before his eyes.

CHAPTER 7

Buchannan Village

"Why are ye smiling? Ye ne'er smile."

Her husband's statement wasn't remotely true. Miren smiled often. Just rarely in front of him.

"Aye, I do. I smile."

"Nae." Her husband's gruff voice sounded pained as he struggled to push himself upright in the bed. "Ye doona."

Miren ignored him as she continued to ready herself for what was sure to be the best day she'd had. This morning, nothing he could say to her would succeed in sinking her spirits. For today and for many moons to come she would be away from her wretch of a husband for most of the waking hours.

"I've already spoken with yer mother. She will come midday with a meal for ye and to help with yer bedpan. Ofrin will be by later, as well, with some tea to help with yer pain and to redress yer wounds. Yer brother will be by this evening with a meal for ye and will keep ye company for a while."

"I forbid ye to go, Miren.

God bless the horse that injured him. It would forever be her favorite creature on earth. She paused, her shoulder catching, as it often did throughout the day—a reminder of the damage her husband could do when on his feet and healthy. Perhaps the bones in his legs wouldn't heal, and he would be bedridden forever.

One could always hope.

But for now, with no use of his legs, he could forbid her nothing, and she would revel in it for as long as she possibly could.

"Murray, ye know that I doona have a choice. Ye canna work while ye are injured, and we must still pay our rents."

"What sort of a laird would see a man out of his home when he canna work through nae fault of his own?"

With her back toward him, Miren rolled her eyes. She'd not been with him when the accident occurred, but she knew his temper. The horse would never have bucked him without cause.

"I doona believe that Laird Buchannan would see us out of our home, but I willna have us take advantage of his kindness when there is something I can do to see our rents paid."

"Yer job is here, with me. I need ye to care for me."

"And I am. All I have done since the day I lost my mind and agreed to marry ye is care for ye. I've seen to it that ye will have people in and out of this house daily to see to ye."

Miren saw the wooden mug hurling toward her in the mirror and ducked out of the way just in time as it smashed into the glass, cracking it down its center.

"I am going, Murray. I willna be back until late. Doona stay up for me."

His nostrils flared and his jaw tightened as she watched him struggle to sit up in the bed.

"My legs will heal, lass, and when they do, ye shall pay for the way ye've disobeyed me."

A familiar fear coursed through her, but she gathered her courage as she pointed to her husband's covered legs.

"Ye've always had shoddy aim, so I doona think yer throwing items at me to be too much of a worry. And from the look of yer legs, even when ye're healed, ye'll be so weak, I doona expect ye'll be able to catch me for a verra long while."

While she managed to keep her voice steady, her hands shook as she reached for her cloak and hurriedly stepped out the door into the cool morning air.

"How do ye intend to manage it, me Lord? I doona mean any offense, but I saw the ladies ye bedded during our travels together. I doona think any of them have the wealth ye are seeking."

Flashes of their escapades together coursed through his mind, filling him with need. Far too much time had passed since he'd been with a woman.

"Davy, for the love o'God, man, ye canna speak of me bedding lassies in the same sentence in which ye call me, 'me Lord.' I insist…nae, I order ye to only call me Paton."

He glanced over at Davy as they rode together into the village to gather Miren and supplies for the castle.

"Fine. If that 'tis what ye wish."

"Aye, 'tis, and ye shouldna disparage the lassies I kept company with, Davy. I canna find fault with any of them."

"Nor can I, but I doona believe I'm wrong when I speak of their lack of wealth. Truly, how do ye intend to find yerself a wealthy wife?"

Little else had occupied his mind since he shook Laird Morton's hand, sealing his fate.

"Bram has helped me come up with a list of all of Scotland's wealthiest lairds who also have eligible daughters. I shall write to each and invite them to visit the isle. The water surrounding us separates us from all but Laird Morton. There are few that have made the journey over to Skye, and many who would wish to see our land if given an excuse to do so. My hope is an invitation will do just that."

"Under what guise?"

"To simply foster kinship and good will between territories. With any luck, they shall bring their daughters and can work on making arrangements once I've worked out which lass would be the least disagreeable."

The village just began to peek its way into view. The distance was farther from the castle than he'd remembered.

"Aye. Why doona ye allow me to see Miren to the castle each morn and escort her back to the village each night? 'Tis a distance the lass shouldna travel alone."

"I doona expect Miren's husband would like the thought of her being alone with any man for such a distance. When we return, I will see if Clara would be willing to travel with ye each way. If so, the two of ye can begin this night."

"I shall be alone with Clara for half of the time. Does that cause no problem?"

Paton chuckled as he leaned forward to pat one of the horses on the rump. "I expect Clara must be older than yer grandmother. I doona believe the two of ye traveling without a chaperone would be viewed in the same way. Besides, the old lass canna keep up with maid duties as she once could. Perhaps helping ye with this task will make her feel useful."

Davy nodded as he pulled on the reigns of the horses as they neared the edge of the village.

"We left the castle earlier than I realized. I expect we will have everything loaded and ready to head back to the castle before midday. Do ye think Miren would mind if we picked her up at her home after we are ready?"

"I doona ken the lass, sir, but I canna see why she would."

Paton nodded. "Then 'tis settled."

"Nae, me Lord. I doona think that 'tis. Look ahead. She awaits us already."

Sure enough, with his gaze now focused in her direction, Paton could make out Miren standing with Seamus.

He called out to her as they approached. "What are ye doing here so early, lass?"

Miren turned toward him, smiling brightly. She looked so much better than she had the night before.

"If ye knew me husband, ye wouldna ask such a question."

Seamus stepped up beside her and pointed to the items behind him. "'Tis all here. Enough to last ye more than a fortnight, I expect."

Before Paton could thank Henry for his quick effort, a familiar, grating voice called to him from behind.

"Laird Buchanna, I dinna expect we would see ye again so soon."

Paton's back tensed as he turned toward Laird Morton.

"I must say the same to ye. Are ye in no hurry to return home? Surely yer castle is more comfortable than our meager inn."

To Paton's dismay, Laird Morton dismounted and walked towards them, his disgusting son right behind him.

"We've found the inn here to be verra fine indeed, although I willna deny how unusual we found it that ye dinna offer us lodging at Buchannan Castle. I expected it rare that any laird is turned away in such a manner. Still, I am glad that our paths have crossed once again."

"Aye? And why is that? I doona think my three months are up yet."

"I only wanted to ask if ye had any objection to my son and I hunting on yer land for a few days before we return home. I shall deduct the worth of anything we kill from the debt ye owe me."

Paton looked over the two scrawny, ill-looking men and smiled. He found it difficult to believe either man decent with a bow and arrow. They'd be lucky if they returned home with a single beast.

"O'course not. And there is no need to deduct anything. I shall come up with the full sum without trouble."

Laird Morton's eyes widened doubtfully. "Yer confidence is larger than yer money satchel, lad."

"Not for long. Now, we must be going. We've much to load. If ye'll excuse us." Paton leaned over to whisper in Davy's ear as they walked away from Laird Morton and his son. "Remind me when we get back to the castle that the invitations to nearby territories need to be sent with a messenger tonight. The quicker this debt is paid, the quicker that miserable sot can be out of our lives for good."

CHAPTER 8

Isle of Skye, Scotland
Present Day

"Rory, get out of the car real fast and warn the people behind us to stay back."

"What?"

Rory turned wide, horrified eyes on me as I cautiously gripped the gear shift.

From what I'd gathered in the few hours I'd had to change our travel plans the next morning, there were two ways one could get over to the Isle of Skye, via ferry boat or bridge. From the location of our hotel—which thankfully had been able to accommodate us earlier than planned—we needed to arrive on Skye via ferry, but we would leave the isle via bridge.

Oh, how I wished we'd chosen to travel via bridge both ways. Every minute of the ferry ride was hell.

The small boat only held twenty cars, tops, and as luck would have it, we arrived smack dab in the middle of the bunch, sandwiched tightly between cars on every side.

Neither of us had ever been on such a rocky boat ride in our life. Car alarms went off as the boat dipped and swayed dramatically to each side with the waves, and more than once I found myself glancing for the location of the lifejackets as I was certain any moment the entire thing was about to capsize.

Clearly though, the Scots were made of stronger stuff than Rory and I, for no one else on the boat seemed worried, and we were the only two that were completely green at the gills by the time we made it to shore.

Sick, shaken, and wet from the numerous sprays of water which seemed to be aimed right at us two foreigners, I returned Rory's shocked expression with an adamant nod.

"You heard me. We are right in the middle of the pack here and everyone is following so close in the line to get off of this boat, yet everyone keeps stopping on this ramp. Not once have I been able to stop this damn vehicle on a hill without rolling backwards when I try to get going again. Go and warn the car behind us to stay back so I don't crash into them and cause a big pileup."

The vision of what was inevitably about to come if Rory didn't do as I asked must've been enough for her to get over her embarrassment, for she jumped out of the car without any further questions.

By the time the line started moving again, she was back.

"Okay, they're going to stay back. I don't think that was the first time they'd dealt with Americans driving over here. They didn't seem the least bit surprised by my request and were more than happy to hold up the line for us."

"Good." I laughed slightly, trying to relieve some of the tension that had built up in both of us over the last hour.

Rory slumped back into the passenger seat as I lurched us forward across the ramp and off the ferry. "This trip is going to get a little less difficult and a little more fun at some point, right?"

"Of course, it is. We're just thrown off because our plans got changed so suddenly, and we are still adjusting to the time change and being in such a new place. Pretty much everything that's gone wrong has involved this dang car and transportation, so hopefully once we make it to the hotel, we can put the car away for a while and explore via foot."

The moment we pulled into the parking lot for the small, six-bedroom inn, I knew our day was about to take another unfortunate turn. The lot was littered with vehicles parked so close together, my only option was to back out of the lot as carefully as I could as a woman in her sixties wearing a backpack ran toward us, flagging us down.

Filled with dread, I lowered the window.

"Ye must be Olivia and Rory, aye? Why doona the two of ye answer yer phones? I've been trying to get hold of ye all day."

Placing the car in park, I reached for my phone and sighed.

"I'm sorry. We've had terrible service for most of our trip. No calls came through."

The woman sighed and extended her hand. "I feared as much. I'm Gladys, the owner here. I know my husband told ye that ye could check in today, and while 'tis true, I'm afraid ye must leave for a while and return after dark. We are in the middle of a private function. Our entire space has been rented out until nine tonight. He should've told ye, and I am so sorry for the trouble."

Releasing my hand, she slipped the backpack off her shoulders and frantically stuffed it through the window and into my lap. "I've packed ye both a right good feast of a picnic. 'Tis a beautiful day, and there is much to explore on the isle. In the front pocket, ye will find brochures for different trailways, or scenic routes, various options with which ye can fill yer day."

Before I could even respond, she began to step away. "I willna charge ye for tonight's stay to make up for the inconvenience. Now, I must get back. I will see the two of ye tonight. Welcome to the Isle of Skye."

She turned and ran back in the direction of the inn as I listened to Rory groan dramatically next to me.

"But I want out of the caaarrr." She dragged the word out like a whiny child, but I didn't have it in me to give her a hard time for it. I felt much the same way.

"Then, let's get out of the car. Let me drive away from this mess of vehicles, and we can look at the brochures and make a plan. We'll go on a hike and a picnic and enjoy the day as much as we can."

Rory nodded, perked up, and reached for her phone. "Fine, but if we are going to be in the car for a while longer, I need something to cheer me up. I'm plugging back in my podcast."

It was my turn to groan. True crime didn't light me up in the same way it did my sister.

"You're twisted, you know that, right? We're in Scotland. We should be listening to bagpipes or something, not to Keith Morrison drone on about murders."

"Keith Morrison doesn't 'drone,' Liv. Give the man some

respect. He could read the phone book and people would listen to it. That voice is like butter."

She wasn't wrong.

"It's not his voice that I'm opposed to. Murder just isn't my thing."

As Keith's voice began reverberating through the car, I accepted my loss and navigated to the nearest pull-off away from the inn, when the words of the old woman I'd met from the night before crossed my mind.

"I know where we should go to explore. Let's navigate over to the Quiraing and drive around until we find a good spot for a picnic. It's supposed to be beautiful."

Rory was too wrapped up in the next shocking twist in the case to answer me, so I proceeded to pull over and look at the map on my own. We were close and I was certain the road we were already on would take us there.

To my delight, it didn't take long once we drove away from the inn for the scenery to become so magnificent that it held even more interest to Rory than the podcast, and she turned off the volume of her own accord.

"Wow. Why did we wait so long to come here?"

Her question made me think of so many things I'd put off in the last handful of years by prioritizing the bakery above all else: romance, friends, travel, children. My priorities had to shift if I didn't want my entire life to pass by without me getting any of the things I truly wanted. I hoped this trip would be the springboard for just such a change.

"Why did we wait so long to do so many things?"

Rory's silence was enough to clue me in on the fact that her thoughts had traveled down the same path. It had been so easy for us to sink into the life our parents had built that we'd both slowly forgotten to build our own.

We continued to drive for a while as we found it difficult to find any spot for a picnic that seemed better than any other. Each mile grew even more breathtaking. Each curve in the road revealed something else magnificent.

In the end, a flock of sheep helped us make the decision. Just at the top of a steep hill in the heart of the Quiraing, we came to find the road completely blocked by a sea of fluff. No other cars were near us, and I couldn't creep forward another inch.

"Think it will be okay for us to park here and hike upwards a little more for a picnic while we wait for them to move along?"

"I can't see why it wouldn't be. It doesn't look as if we will be moving anywhere for a while. Just be careful getting out on your side. You're pretty close to the edge there."

Turning the ignition off, I reached for the backpack and slipped it over my shoulders as I stepped out into the crisp, Scottish air. The bag was heavier than I'd expected, and it threw my balance off just enough to really draw my attention to how close I actually was to the edge of the cliff.

"You're right. The road couldn't be any closer to the edge here without just crumbling."

"Yeah, be careful. Move over to this side by coming around the front. Don't worry about the sheep. I think they're pretty docile. Come over here on my side, and we can trek up the hill together. It looks like there's a flat patch not too far away from the sheep where we could set up lunch."

Everything happened so quickly after that. Before I could respond to Rory—before I could even take a step forward into the flock of sheep—Rory threw her arms over her head and squealed as she stretched.

Something caught in my chest the moment I heard the noise, as if I could sense the panic it sent in the sheep surrounding me. In flash, the flock shifted, pushing into me as I lost my balance and fell backwards over the side of the cliff.

The last thing I heard was the sound of Rory screaming as I made impact with the first rock on the way down and everything went black.

CHAPTER 9

Isle of Eight Lairds, Scotland
17th Century

"Breathe, lass. Come, and let me hold ye. At least try to get some more sleep. We canna head out until dawn."

Kate sighed and rolled over into the crook of her husband's arm. She knew he was right. Sleep was what she needed the most but for weeks now it hadn't come easily. All she could think about was Paton.

After years of waiting, his time with the fae had come to an end. The sentence he'd paid in her place was over.

She should be thrilled. Why then did a lump settle deep into her stomach every time she thought about him coming home?

She couldn't place her finger on it, but something didn't sit well. Whatever their expectations for how the day would go, she knew the fae would make sure to surprise them in some way. They would keep their word, but only as much as they absolutely had to. Anything in their agreement that could be misinterpreted, they would exploit.

There was no chance of the day going as planned.

"Do you think he's okay?"

Maddock squeezed her, kissing the top of her hair as they snuggled close in the darkness.

"Aye, lass. Paton is strong. He willna be the same lad he was going in, I am certain, but whatever demons haunt him now, we will help him through it once he is home. He wouldna want ye missing sleep over him."

Kate let out one more long, stressed breath as she rolled over and listened to the sound of her husband blissfully slipping back to sleep.

Whether Paton wished it or not, much sleep had been missed due to her worry for him since the day he took her place in the fae's realm. She saw no reason why the habit was finally going to break itself right now.

Every terrible scenario possible played itself over and over in her mind as she willed the sun to rise more quickly.

"He's gone."

Kate's hands trembled, and her throat began to close from panic in response to the fae's words.

Shakily, she took one step toward the formidable creature.

"What do you mean, 'he's gone'?"

Machara's father smiled, his lips pulling back in a way that made it impossible for him to pass as human. The otherworldly creature crossed his arms and casually shrugged.

"I mean precisely what I said. He's gone. We grew bored of him over a year ago."

"You swore that he would be returned safely." Kate's voice broke as tears pooled in her eyes.

"I've not broken my promise. As I said, we grew bored of him and released him from our realm long ago. It was his decision to leave the isle. Once free of us, we did nothing to help nor hinder where he wished to go. He chose to leave."

Kate gasped as relief flooded her system. It didn't make sense that Paton would leave here, but at least he was alive.

"Where is he?"

The fae laughed and turned to leave.

"Do you really think I would keep track of any human once I'm finished with them? He could be anywhere. Find him yourself."

And with that, the fae was gone, and so, apparently, was Paton.

CHAPTER 10

Isle of Skye, Scotland
17th Century

"Do ye think she's dead?"

"Nae. Are ye daft? Canna ye see that she's breathing? Look at her chest."

"Why is she dressed so?"

"How would I know? I doona know the lass any more than ye do."

"Is she a whore?"

"I wouldna doubt it. She looks as if she could be one."

"Do we leave her?"

"The lass is fair enough. Mayhap if we show her some kindness, she may be apt to repay it."

I tried to open my eyes, but my body resisted as I listened to the set of strange voices speak over me. Where was I? What had happened? My mind struggled to regain its grip on reality, and I didn't fight as I felt the two strangers lift me by my feet and shoulders and carry me away from wherever I was laying.

They lifted me with ease, and as I listened to the crunch of the ground beneath their boots, everything came flooding back.

The hill. The sheep. Rory's squeal.

I'd fallen off the side of a cliff.

How was I possibly still alive?

Furthermore, while my head ached dreadfully, the rest of my body wasn't in excruciating pain. Every bone in my body should've been broken from that fall.

Was I paralyzed?

No. I could feel one of the man's hands on my shoulders, and I could feel the other man's hands around my ankles.

What in the hell had happened?

Only once the men stopped moving and I was placed back on the ground did I attempt to open my eyes again. This time, I was able to slowly flicker my eyes open.

"Och, there ye are, lass. What happened to ye? Are ye well enough to speak?"

I nodded, which caused me to reach up and grip the sides of my head in pain. At least I was now certain I could move my arms. Groaning, I pushed myself up into a sitting position as I looked my rescuers over for the first time.

The men were dressed strangely, each in a kilt and a heavy coat. They looked like they'd just left some sort of reenactment or cosplay convention.

"I…I fell." I paused and gently moved my head around to take in my surroundings. "I pointed to the top of the hill. "From up there."

The oldest man laughed and shook his head. "Nae, I doona think 'tis possible, lass. Ye wouldna have survived a fall like that."

I agreed. But somehow I had.

"Why are the two of you dressed like that? Is there some sort of convention going on?"

The youngest man furrowed his brows at me as he crouched down close. "How did ye get over to the isle, lass? Ye are no' from here. I can tell that much by the way ye speak."

I bent my knees and carefully pushed myself up until I was standing. Sure enough, no broken bones. Just some scrapes here and there and a wicked bad headache. I probably had a concussion.

"No. I'm from Seattle, and we took the ferry boat over. Do either of you have a car? I have to make it back up to the top of the Quiraing. My sister must be hysterical. There's no way she doesn't think I'm dead. And I probably need to go to a hospital to get my head checked out."

The two men stared at me blankly for a long moment. I decided to continue.

"I appreciate your help, but I really could use a lift. I…I can pay you for your trouble once I make it back to our rental car."

The younger man turned to look at the man I assumed was his father. "The lass is daft in her head. She speaks utter nonsense."

Ignoring me, the older stranger turned his back completely toward me as he leaned in toward the other man and spoke in a whisper.

After a moment, he faced me once again. "What is yer name, lass?"

"Olivia Bailey. May I ask yours? Also, do either one of you have some water and maybe a pain killer or two?"

"Lass, my name is Laird Morton, and this is my son, Lanrick." He paused long enough to step forward and grab me by one arm as his son stepped toward me to grab my other. I tried to pull away, but I wasn't strong enough to resist. "I doona want ye to resist, but I must insist that my son and I see ye back into the village and find whoever 'tis ye belong to. Every village has a mad woman or two. There is no shame in it."

I panicked and yanked and pulled as they dragged me, but my arms were quickly pulled behind my back and tied together with rope.

"Wait. What are you doing? I'm not…I'm not crazy. And what village? I don't belong to anyone. Just let me go. I don't need your help. I can find my way back on my own."

"We intend to hunt in these woods, lass. Ye shall scare the animals away, and I doona trust that ye wouldna kill us as we slept. We will see ye back to the village so ye may be locked up wherever 'twas ye escaped from."

My head throbbed as my feet were forced to stumble along with the terrible men. When they stopped short in front of two horses, my confusion grew. I twisted frantically to look around me, but I could see no roadways or cars, only a small, dirt path snaking its way through the trees.

"I didn't escape from anywhere! Wait! You really don't have cars?"

Neither man answered me as they hoisted me up on top of one of the horses and the son climbed on top of the creature behind me.

"Just sit still, lass, and we willna give ye any trouble. 'Tis no' far to the village."

Laird Morton mounted his own horse and called after his son.

"Do ye have her well in hand, lad? If so, I shall ride fast ahead and try to find the wench's home."

Lanrick screamed far too close to my ear. "Aye, she willna go anywhere now. We shall meet ye there."

Laird Morton rode away from us without another word.

My head needed tending to, I needed to find Rory, but I also knew that I was at a disadvantage here. I had no idea what sort of nonsense these men thought about me, but if he really did intend to bring me into any sort of village, surely this entire incident would come to an end there. I couldn't imagine that any town would be okay with a man riding into town with a bound woman on horseback. Someone would save me then.

"Yer master hurt ye, aye? And ye ran? Ye do know that we are surrounded by water, doona ye, lass? I doona know where ye thought ye would go."

"My master? I'm not married, and even if I was, I hardly think the man would be my master."

Lanrick's horse trotted along slowly as his arms tightened around me.

"I dinna say I thought ye were married. Whores rarely are."

"Excuse me?" I could feel Lanrick's breath on my neck, and a terrifying dread settled into my gut. "I am not a whore."

"A lady of the night then, aye? Mayhap ye serve the leisure of Laird Buchannan? Mayhap yer father has an arrangement with him? I've heard of the new laird's appetite for women, and I saw full well his temper only a few nights ago. He shoulda have hit ye, lass. I ne'er treat those that serve me in such a way."

He pulled the horse to a stop and fear clutched at my throat as I felt Lanrick dismount the horse and reach for my waist.

"Ye are prettier than the whores in our territory, though I can barely stand to look at the way ye are dressed. I'll be gentler than Laird Buchannan was, lass. As long as ye oblige me, I willna hurt ye a bit."

I wanted to scream, but like in a terrible nightmare where your voice evades you, I couldn't get any sound to escape as he pulled me down from the horse and led me to a tree. My breath came ragged and shaky as I closed my eyes and tried to think.

Lanrick moved toward me quickly. His kilt hiked up as he neared me, and I backed up into the tree behind me.

"Remove yer breeches, lass."

My voice shook as I spoke. "I…I can't. My hands are tied."

He growled, allowing his kilt to drop as his hands moved to my waist. He fumbled with the belt on my jeans as tears sprung up in my eyes.

"You'll….you'll have to remove my sneakers. They're skinny jeans. They can't be pulled off over my shoes."

Lanrick groaned in annoyance and dropped to his knees to fumble with my shoes as I took a shaky breath to steady myself. With his eye level with my knee, I thrust my knee upward into his head, knocking him unsteady before I lifted my foot and kicked him with as much force as I could manage right in the center of his chest.

He fell backwards and his head made a terrible cracking sound as it hit the base of the tree. It only took seconds for the grass underneath his head to turn crimson as I watched his eyes go blank.

I screamed in horror as I bent in front of him, and he took his last raspy breath.

I'd killed him.

Shaking, I pushed myself to my feet and blindly ran into the woods.

Please let this be a dream. Please let me still be unconscious.

I played the prayer over and over in my mind as I ran and stumbled with my arms still tied behind me, but deep down I knew the truth. I was very much awake, and every bit of this nightmare was real.

CHAPTER 11

Paton loved the feel of the wind brushing past him when he truly let his horse run. He glanced over his shoulder to see his sister following closely behind. She was a fine rider.

At Ella's bequest, they'd bundled up early in the morning and prepared for a day away from the castle spent riding and exploring the isle. It was long past time for him to do so. While the occasional trip into the village was a necessary evil, Paton knew he'd allowed himself to become far too much of a hermit since his return home.

As the sound of hooves approached, Paton pulled the reins of his horse to slow its speed so that Ella could catch him.

"Bram ne'er allows me to ride so recklessly. He is endlessly worried that I'll hurt meself."

"Bram's lost much, lass. He only cares for ye. But ye are an expert rider. He has no reason to be worried."

He didn't miss her smile as she sat up a little straighter.

"Aye, 'tis exactly what I've been telling him for ages."

They rode quietly for a time, each enjoying the scenery as their horses recovered from their run. But even in the short time he'd known her, Paton could tell when his sister wished to talk.

"So…do ye intend to tell me what 'tis ye wish to speak to me about, or will we waste the day in silence?"

"'Tis it no' possible that I only wished to spend time with ye?"

He shook his head. "I doona believe so, sister. History says otherwise."

He could sense her hesitancy and tried to encourage her further. "I doona bite, lass. What is it?"

"Bram told me something about ye. I'm no' certain I believe him, and I doona want ye to laugh at me if he was only trying to make me look a fool."

Suspecting he already knew what piece of Paton's past Bram had divulged, Paton pulled his horse to a stop and dismounted.

"Why doona we stop for a bit? We can rest in the grass while ye ask me. I promise ye I willna laugh."

"Verra well."

Paton pulled a blanket from his horse's pack and spread it out on the ground for them before reaching for apples to snack on while Ella took her time seeing to her horse. Once she joined him, it took her no time to work up her nerve.

"Did ye truly once have magical powers? Bram swears that ye did, but I am no' so sure that magic even exists."

Yes. He'd been correct in his assumptions. He rarely thought about his old powers now—he did his best not to—but he couldn't blame his sister for asking. He supposed she deserved the truth. Perhaps, it would help her to better understand why he'd left their family so long ago.

"Believe it or no', Bram spoke truthfully. I did once possess magic, but I no longer do. I no longer know of any that do."

Ella's eyes widened as she bit into her apple, and with a full mouth begged him to continue.

"Tell me everything."

And so he did. For the first time since leaving the land of the fae, he told another his story. The whole truth of it, without mincing even the most painful of parts. He told her of Nicol's arrival on the isle and how the magic inside him had called him to go with the old laird who needed his assistance. He told her of the lassies from another time who'd befriended him and what he'd sacrificed to help his dear friend.

He spoke of the fae and how his years with them changed him. How they'd toyed with him, torturing him and allowing him pleasure in a dizzying mix that nearly drove him mad. And how one day, they'd come to him unbidden and granted him his freedom.

"But why brother? If they sought to drive ye to madness, why would they give ye yer freedom?"

Everything inside of him wanted to cut his story short, to end his tale there and not proceed further, but someone other than him needed to know. Someone needed to hear the names of all those he'd loved so deeply.

"Because, lass, they knew that once I learned of what had befallen Nicol's men and the time traveling women who loved them, that grief would make faster work of the job."

Ella swallowed, her voice unsteady, as she asked, "Wh…what happened to them?"

"To this day, I doona know what happened. While I would

love to blame the fae, for at least then I would have someone to seek vengeance against, I doona believe the crimes that were committed against them to be the fae's way of meddling in the human world. I doona know why or who did it, but every single person I knew and loved at the castle was killed. I saw their lifeless bodies with me own eyes."

"Oh, brother." Tears fell down Ella's cheeks as she reached for his hand. "How did ye survive it? What did ye do?"

"For a long while, I dinna think I would. I almost threw meself off the cliffside so that the ocean would take me and end the ache inside of me, but then I thought of ye and Bram, and Ma and Da, and I couldna do it. Instead, I spent many months in a stupor, traveling anywhere but home as I worked and philandered me way around Scotland. When hard labor and loose women dinna heal the pain, I knew that there was no reason to stay away from home any longer."

Silently, Ella rose onto her knees and leaned toward him, wrapping her arms over his shoulders as she drew him in close.

"It's okay to cry brother. I willna tell a soul."

And so he wept in his sister's arms until finally his tears ran dry and his soul felt just a little bit lighter. At least now, all of the pain and sadness wasn't his to carry alone.

Where could they possibly be? Sure, he'd expected Lanrick to have his way with the lass. That was part of the reason he'd ridden ahead of them, but no lass could keep a man pleased for this long.

To make matters worse, none in the village seemed to know of the strange woman they'd found. Did Buchannan territory really not keep whores? And if not, where else could the woman have come from?

The village truly was hell. He would change that with time. Once Lanrick and Lady Ella Buchannan were wed, he would make quick work of seeing Paton and Bram to their graves, then the entire isle would be his.

Laird Morton paced the village tavern as his patience grew thin, and dusk began to set over the horizon. Throwing back the rest of his drink, he returned to his horse to ride back into the woods.

The ride was short, and an uneasiness settled over him with each stretch of road he traveled without meeting up with his son and the idiot whore.

A sound of neighing in the distance caught his attention as he directed the horse off the path and toward the sound. His pulse quickened as Lanrick's riderless steed came into view, and he dismounted with urgency as he ran toward the animal. He spun around frantically in search of his son, and as his eyes panned downward, he dropped to his knees as he began to wail.

The bitch had killed his only son and heir.

CHAPTER 12

Perhaps I really was the insane woman my captors had thought me to be. With each passing minute, I questioned my sanity further. For hours, I'd wandered aimlessly through the dense trees, and not once had I come across a person who could help me. Even more strangely, I'd seen nothing that resembled the landscape Rory and I had passed through—no cars, or gas stations, no paved roads, nothing.

My head still ached dreadfully, and I could no longer feel my arms. And my legs wouldn't stop shaking from shock.

Just when I was about to collapse from exhaustion, I stumbled out onto a dirt road where I thought I could hear voices in the distance.

I listened quietly for a moment to ensure the voice didn't sound like Laird Morton's. When the sound of female laughter reached my ears, I began to scream for help. Seconds later, two horses pulling an open cart came rolling toward me. As it slowed to a stop, I dropped to my knees in such deep relief that

I didn't even have the energy to process or care just how weird it was that people had just arrived via such an ancient form of transportation.

"Oh my God, Davy. Help the poor lass into the back. She looks as if she is near death."

I didn't think I was actually in that bad of shape, but I had no doubt I looked it.

"Please, please untie my hands. I can't feel them."

I looked up just as the man holding the horse's reins jumped down to assist me. It only took seconds for him to pull a blade from his kilt and slice the rope so that my arms were set free. Both arms fell limply to my sides, and I groaned in pain.

"Och, lass, what has happened to ye?"

Before I could answer, the man wrapped an arm around my waist to help me into the wagon as one of the two women crawled into the back with me.

She immediately reached out and began massaging one of my arms up and down to help with blood flow.

"How long were ye tied, lass?"

"Several hours. Listen, I…I have to get back to the top of the Quiraing and find my sister. She'll know what to do. Whether I need a hospital or a lawyer so I don't get arrested for murder or…?"

"Murder, lass?" The woman dropped her hands and regarded me nervously.

Shit, I thought to myself. I'd just admitted to manslaughter in front of total strangers.

"I…I didn't mean to. He was going to rape me. I just kicked him so I could get away. I didn't know that he would fall and crack his head like that."

The woman sighed and reached for my arm again.

"Alright, take a breath, lass. Ye are safe now. We will see ye into the village. There is a healer there who can see to yer wounds. Then we can see about finding yer sister, and ye can tell us the whole story."

Panic shot through me like lightning as I jerked away from her and tried to stand, but the fast movement made me dizzy, and I collapsed back down on my bottom.

Laird Morton was in the village. I couldn't risk seeing him.

"No! I can't go to the village. Please just take me back up into the Quiraing and help me find my sister."

"Lass, we must see yer wounds tended to before we do anything else, and I canna do that here."

I tried to stand again, but she kept her grip on my arm, her voice stern as she spoke to me again.

"Listen to me, lass. Look into me eyes. My name is Miren. I, nor anyone else here, will harm ye. If ye truly willna go to the village, we will turn around and take ye to the castle, aye? I am no' a healer, but mayhap I can tend to yer wounds for tonight, at least. But I willna permit us to go in search of anyone else until I know ye are well. Do ye understand?"

Rory desperately needed to know I was okay, but for the moment, I knew Miren was right. My head wounds needed cleaning, and I needed some water quickly or I feared I would pass out from dehydration. There was no way that Rory didn't believe me dead. Chances were authorities were already gathered searching for my body near where I'd fallen. The isle wasn't that huge. Surely word would spread of a missing woman, and she would find me sooner or later.

I nodded, and the wagon suddenly started moving.

"Has the castle been converted into a hospital or something?"

Miren ran her hand up and down my arm soothingly as if I were a small child babbling total nonsense.

"Lass, I doona know what a hospital is." She paused and opened her arms to me. "Why doona ye lay yer head in my lap and rest for the journey? Ye sound as if ye might need a good sleep."

Logically, I knew that the last thing I should do with a head injury was sleep, but as Miren gently pulled me toward her, all of the adrenaline drained from my body, and I could do nothing else but surrender myself to darkness.

I woke as the small buggy we rode in rolled to a stop and Miren gave my shoulders a gentle shake.

"We're here, lass. Clara has run ahead to ready a bath and a bed for ye. Davy and I will help ye inside. Once ye've cleaned yerself up a bit, I'll come in and see if I can see to yer wounds, aye?"

Groggily, I nodded as I tried to make out my surroundings in the moonlight. "Okay."

The two of them gently helped me down, and Davy kept his arm supportively around me as we ventured inside the castle. Candles scattered the entryway, and I looked up in awe. I'd expected my first trip to a Scottish castle to involve a ticket booth and audio guide, not that I'd be escorted in by two of its residents.

"Do you not have electricity?"

Miren walked ahead of us, but she glanced over her shoulder at my question.

"Och, lass, we mayhap need to send for the healer tonight. It seems as if ye are speaking a language entirely of yer own making."

I hadn't a clue how to respond to that. Rather than say anything that would only further add to their suspicion that I had lost my mind, I remained silent as we walked through the long, dimly lit corridor.

With the buggy, the low lighting in the castle, and the outfits of those escorting me, I couldn't shake the feeling that something about this felt like an entirely different time period. Was this castle like some sort of Colonial Williamsburg, where the workers dressed in period clothes and the authentic representation was part of the bit? It had to be, but I still thought the lack of motorized transportation or electricity seemed a bit extreme.

When we finally reached the door at the end of the long hallway, Miren opened it and stepped aside so Davy could escort me in. The room was more brightly lit than the others, as a fire crackled in a small fireplace in the corner of the room and candles lit each piece of furnishing. But with the extra light, I could see how neglected the room truly was. Dust covered everything, and cobwebs hung high up on the ceiling. Miren must've seen my expression for she reached for my hand as Davy finally relaxed his grip.

"Doona fash, lass. I'll work on beating the bed linens while ye bathe. I'm certain Clara cleaned the tub before beginning her work of heating the water. The castle is no' used to guests, and I doona expect any room, save Bram and the laird's, would be in better condition."

"The laird's?" Had my insistence that they avoid the village delivered me right inside Laird Morton's home? "Is this…is this Laird Morton's home?"

Miren's expression shifted again, back to one of concern. "Nae, lass. Do ye truly no' know where ye are? Laird Morton owns the other half of the isle. Ye are on the Buchannan clan half, in Buchannan Castle."

I let out an audible sigh of relief, and it was only then that I took notice of the large tub situated near the fire.

"No running water either? What about toilets? You've got to have toilets, right?"

Ignoring me, Miren brushed past me, her voice low as she spoke to Davy. I could still hear every word she said.

"Davy, I think I should stay with the lass. Will ye ride back into the village and give word to my husband? Doona tell him about our new guest. Simply tell him that my duties require that I stay too late for me to travel home this eve. He willna be pleased, but there is naught he can do about it for now. And afterwards, please fetch the healer, Nina. I think we shouldna wait til morning to have the lassie's head seen to."

I turned toward the sound of footsteps as Clara entered the room, a large steaming bucket in tow.

"Don't you think it would be better if you just took me to a hospital? I might need an MRI or something to check for a brain bleed."

I was met with glazed, confused expressions.

"It will take Clara some time to fill the bath, lass. In the meantime, I think it best we take ye to see Paton. Are ye ready to meet the laird?" She reached for my hand as she quickly leaned toward Davy. "Leave now, lad. And ride as quickly as ye can."

CHAPTER 13

The knock on his bedchamber door startled him. Although it was still early in the evening, the day spent riding had tired him.

Rising nude from his bed, Paton reached for his kilt, lazily wrapping it around his waist before loosely pinning it so that it only covered his most intimate areas. Miren was gone for the day, and Ella had long since retired, as well. Surely, it was Bram or Davy that awaited him on the other side of the door, and neither man would be offended by the bareness of his body.

Instead, Paton opened the door to find, not one, but two women staring back at him.

"I am so verra sorry to disturb ye, but I thought it best we seek yer council. We nearly ran over the lass…"

Paton could no longer hear Miren's voice as he looked the other woman over.

A lass from the future. There was no question about it. From the excessive way she painted her face to the abundance of a fabric Kate referred to as denim stretched over her legs, he knew the lass wasn't from this time.

"How did ye get here, lass?" He'd been certain he would never see another time-traveler again.

Miren stopped talking and reached out to place her hand on the lass' shoulder.

"I was just telling ye, Paton. I think she needs our assistance. She's been injured. We found her on the road."

"Nae!" He shook his head, brushing Miren's comments away. "I doona mean, how did ye get to this castle, lass, I mean, how did ye get to this time?"

"What?" The woman's voice was soft and unsure. It took no time for Miren to speak up for the girl once again.

"Paton, what is the matter with ye? Ye are no' listening to a word I'm telling ye. Are ye drunk?"

A flurry of emotions coursed through him as he stared into the eyes of the still-nameless woman. Was she a friend of Kate's or perhaps Laurel's? Had she come all this way to find her friends? God, how he hoped not. He didn't think he could bear to retell his tale another time today.

But Miren was right. The woman clearly did need their assistance, and his questioning of her would have to wait.

"Forgive me, Miren. Ye are right. We need to get the healer from the village."

Miren nodded. "Aye. Davy is already on his way. We've readied the room at the end of the hall for the lass, and Clara is drawing her a bath. I think she's injured in her mind, Paton. She speaks of things that I know no' of."

Paton couldn't suppress a smile as memories of Laurel's sudden appearance on the Isle of Eight Lairds crossed his mind and what an adjustment it had been for them all.

"Aye, I'm sure ye canna, but I doona think the lass is mad. See to her bath and pull some of mother's gowns out for the lass to wear. Allow me to properly dress meself, and I will join ye all once the healer arrives, aye?"

Shutting the door between them, Paton quickly unpinned his kilt and went to the work of donning it correctly. He could barely wait to speak to the lass. Just looking at her made him feel at home.

I waited until Clara finished preparing my bath and I was left alone inside the bedroom with Miren to speak again. The period of silence allowed me time to think through all that had happened over the span of the day, but no matter how many times I thought through everything, I struggled to explain it.

The fall should've killed me, or at least left me in far worse condition than I was now. How had it not?

I also knew that it made absolutely no sense that the only people I'd come across in Scotland since my fall didn't seem to understand words like 'car,' or 'hospital.' While I was by no means well-traveled, I knew enough to know that Scotland had pretty much the exact same conveniences in their everyday lives as we had. How did one explain that?

Furthermore, my mind still wrestled to come to terms with the undeniable fact that I'd killed someone. I couldn't bring myself to feel guilty about it. Killing him hadn't been my intention, and if I hadn't done something, the man would've undoubtedly raped me. But the knowledge that another's life had ended because of my actions still made me feel so ill that every time I allowed my mind to think about it, I had to swallow hard to keep from vomiting.

Lastly, what in the world had the handsome laird meant by asking me how I arrived in this time? I knew I'd not misheard him. I'd seen Miren's baffled expression to his question, as well.

I knew it was likely that I had a concussion. Could that be muddling my mind and causing nothing to make sense?

A thought occurred to me for the first time, and I couldn't understand why I'd not asked for one before.

"Miren, I know you're probably not allowed to have it while you're working, but seeing as I know my sister for sure has first responders looking for me all over the isle, would it be possible for me to borrow your personal cell phone to call her? Once I'm back with her, I'll pay you for the cost of it since you'll be dialing an overseas number."

She sighed as she walked across the rooms and reached for my hands as she leaned in close to lock eyes with my own.

"Ye are frightening me, lass. I doona know what a 'cell phone' is. I doona feel comfortable leaving ye in this room alone while ye bathe, but I shall turn away from ye if ye wish for privacy while ye undress."

No. I grew more certain with each passing second. My mind wasn't muddled. I wasn't misunderstanding Miren's genuine concern for me. And I didn't believe the woman was acting. She wasn't committing to her Williamsburg bit so fully that she was lying to me when she was worried for my welfare. She truly didn't know what the things I'd mentioned were.

The laird's question rose to the forefront of my mind once again as I spoke the impossible and pointless question out loud.

"Miren, what century are we in?

She frowned at me again. “Oh, ye sweet, poor, lass. Do ye truly no’ know?”

Hesitantly, I answered her, as a strange knowing settled inside me. It made absolutely no sense, but I could no longer come to any other conclusion that could explain any of the events past the time of my fall. Somehow, through my tumble, I’d crossed through some veil and ended up in an entirely different time.

“We’re not in the twenty-first century, are we, Miren?”

Miren shook her head as she pulled me into a pitiful hug. “Nae, lass. We are in the seventeenth.”

CHAPTER 14

Despite Miren's unwavering gaze as I soaked in the warm bath, cleaning myself did wonders for my nerves. Despite how unbelievable my circumstances, finding an explanation helped calm my panic.

Only Rory weighed heavily on my mind. I knew she would be devastated over my assumed death, but oddly enough, knowing that it was impossible for me to reach her right now allowed me to relax just a little.

Eventually, I would find a way back. If it was possible to fall backwards in time, there had to be a way to go forward. I would find it, and in time, Rory and I would both recover from the trauma of our strange Scottish trip from hell. In the meantime, I knew the best thing I could possibly do for myself was to tend to my injuries and try to make allies that could protect me from the inevitable wrath of Laird Morton.

"How are ye feeling, lass? Ye look better. I've always thought there are few things a good hot bath canna do. If ye are up to it, let's get ye dried off and dressed. I doona think it should be long before Davy arrives back with the healer."

Nodding, I reached for the fabric that felt nothing like a towel and wrapped it around me as I stepped out of the tub.

"I feel much better. I truly don't think I need a healer. My headache has even eased quite a bit."

"All the same, ye shall see one. Here, lass, let us slip this sleeping gown onto ye and get ye settled into the bed."

I obliged her, and with perfect timing, there was a knock at the door as soon as I'd situated myself into a sitting position in bed.

Laird Buchannan entered along with an elderly woman with long, wispy white hair carrying a satchel. Without his chiseled, bare chest as a distraction, I was able to convince my eyes to wander over the rest of him. He was tall, with broad shoulders and a slim waist, and his hair was dark and short. He smiled kindly at me, and his left cheek dimpled in the cutest way. I found it impossible not to smile back at him. He was the most breathtaking man I'd seen in ages.

"Ye are smiling, lass. The bath must've done ye some good, aye?"

"It helped tremendously. Thank you. Everyone truly has been so kind."

He shook his head, brushing away my thanks. "I'm certain Miren has been glad to help. It has kept her away from home."

Miren laughed and rose from her spot next to me on the bed. "He isna wrong, lass. Though I may no' be glad for it whenever I do make it back there. My husband willna be pleased."

The dread in her voice made me uncomfortable, but I had

no opportunity to respond to her as Laird Buchannan ushered the old woman over to my side.

"Nina doesna speak, lass, but she is a fine healer. Drink whatever 'tis she gives ye, let her place whatever salve she wishes to use, and ye shall feel better for it, I promise."

The old woman worked quickly, looking me over as she moved her hands to my face to examine the various scratches I'd acquired from my fall. Rummaging through her bag, she pulled out a small glass jar filled with a foul-smelling substance which she smeared over each small scrape. Afterwards, she motioned for something, and Miren returned shortly with a glass of water which the old woman dumped a powdered substance into before giving it a stir with her slender finger. She extended it to me, and I drank. It tasted of flowers and something akin to mud.

Once I forced myself to swallow the last drop, the old woman stood, closed her bag, and gave me a gentle nod before leaving. Laird Buchannan ushered her out into the hallway before returning to address Miren.

"Clara has made up another bedchamber for ye, lass. Go and get ye some rest. I shall sit with our new guest for a while."

Miren looked at me, her eyes hesitant. "I doona know if 'tis proper for ye to be alone with the lass while she is in bed. I doona mind staying with her."

Laird Buchannan smiled at me in a knowing way that made it seem like I'd known him for far longer than a few minutes. After the last time I'd been alone with a man that day, it would've made perfect sense for me to be hesitant to be alone with one again, but no part of me felt unsafe in his presence.

"I doona think this lass will be as worried about what may or may not be proper than as most. I wish to speak with her alone, Miren. I shall explain all to ye come morning. I give ye me word."

Miren waited until I gave her a permissive nod before giving my foot a gentle squeeze through the blankets and leaving us alone in the room. Once the door latched behind her, Laird Buchannan spoke again.

"Mayhap we should begin with our names, aye? I'm Paton. And ye are?"

He moved to drag a chair from across the room nearer to me as I answered him. "I'm Olivia, but everyone calls me Liv."

"'Tis lovely to meet ye, Liv. I apologize for me rudeness earlier. As usual, Miren was right. Me first concern should have been yer well-being. 'Tis only that I have no' been around a lassie like ye for a verra long time."

"A lassie like me?"

He crossed his arms and regarded me with the same knowing expression. "From the future, lass. I know ye are'na from this time."

"How exactly do you know that? I've only very recently figured that out myself."

He frowned and leaned forward in his chair. "Ye mean that ye dinna come here on purpose, lass? Ye are'na in search of Laurel or Kate?"

I shook my head and immediately regretted the motion. While my head pain had subsided some, it certainly wasn't completely gone.

"I don't know anyone of either name. And I assure you I didn't come here on purpose."

He appeared to be both surprised and relieved by my answer as he relaxed his stance and crossed his arms in front of him.

"So, why doona ye tell me what happened, lass? Start from the beginning."

I supposed it made sense that if I had somehow come upon some sort of strange time portal, that others would have, as well. And I found it immensely reassuring that I was not the first such person Paton knew. It meant I could tell him the truth and he would believe me. Hopefully, he would even be willing to help me find my way back home.

Taking a big breath to settle myself, I began. I told him of the trip we'd planned and how both Rory and I were reluctant to travel to Scotland. I even went into an excessive amount of detail about how much I hated our car. And I told him of how I'd fallen and woken up in the presence of two men in a time entirely different from my own.

Only then did he interrupt me. "So the fall sent ye back here, then?"

I shrugged. "It had to. One second, I was in my own time, then I fell, and suddenly I wasn't."

He frowned at me and bit his lip in a way that suddenly made the room feel warm.

"I've ne'er heard of anyone traveling back in such a way."

"Well, every bit of this is new to me, so all I can tell you is what happened to me."

"O'course, lass. Please continue."

"When I opened my eyes, there were two men with me, but unlike yourself they seemed to be quite unfamiliar with people from my time. They thought I was a whore. They thought I was out of my mind. They bound my wrists and kidnapped me, insisting they would see me back into the village. But then, one of the men rode ahead and the other…"

Just as I was about to get to the most distressing part of my day, the door swung open behind Paton as a man I'd yet to see burst inside.

"Paton, ye must come. Laird Morton is here. I doona think I've ever seen a man more distraught. His son is dead, and he insists that someone in this territory killed him."

My breath caught in my throat. "Paton, wait!" I tried to call out to him, but he was already out the door.

Crap. Throwing back the covers, I ran frantically around the room in search of my sneakers, as I tried to think of any way I could escape the castle without being found by Laird Morton.

CHAPTER 15

"What do ye mean his son is dead? And murdered no less? Surely, he must be mistaken."

Paton hurried alongside his brother down the long hallway.

"I doona know, brother. I only know what the man told me. I dinna permit him to speak long. I knew I needed to get ye."

"Wait!"

Miren's voice called out to him, and there was a desperation in her tone that stopped him mid stride.

"Bram, go and tell Laird Morton that I am coming. Get the man a drink and see him to the sitting room."

As his brother ran ahead, Miren stepped in close, her voice nearly a whisper.

"Ye must not tell Laird Morton of our guest upstairs. Doona let him see ye know anything about her"

Paton frowned. "Why? What does she have to do with any of this?"

Miren sighed and leaned in closer. "I am no' certain, but I

think it might have been she who killed Laird Morton's son."

"What?" The very idea seemed impossible to him. The poor lass hadn't even been in this century for a single day. How could she possibly have committed any such crime so quickly?

"When we found the lass, she was shaking from head to toe and her hands were bound behind her back, Paton. She freely told us that she'd just killed a man, but 'twas unintentional. The man tried to rape her."

Paton's jaw clenched at the thought of anyone laying unwanted hands on a woman, but he knew enough of Lanrick Morton to believe him capable of such a heinous act.

"Did she say 'twas Lanrick?"

"Nae, but when I referred to ye as laird, I saw the panic in her eyes, Paton. She thought I meant Laird Morton. She believed we'd brought her back to his home. We must protect her. If she did kill him, I believe there was reason for it."

"Aye. Go and see to the lass at once. Doona leave her alone. I fear she might try to run in her haste to avoid any interaction with Thayne. I will come up with something to tell him. Thank ye, Miren. For everything ye've done this night."

Lanrick deserved what he got. Paton could bring himself to feel no sadness for the man's death as he made his way down to the sitting room where Laird Morton awaited him. Whatever he needed to do to protect the time-traveling lass, he would do so.

"Laird Morton, Bram has told me what has happened. I am so verra sorry."

The lie was a necessary one. He would have to tread carefully to avoid Laird Morton taking his vengeance out on the entire territory.

Laird Morton stood, his face red, his teeth bared in anger.

"I've only come to ask ye two questions. First, was it ye that sent the lass to do this? Did ye have my son murdered so that yer sister wouldna have to wed him?"

Keeping his expression calm, Paton moved across the room to sit in the chair opposite Thayne.

"'Tis grief that has made ye ask such a question. Ye know verra well that I had nothing to do with this. And if I were to wish someone killed, I wouldna send another to do the job for me."

Laird Morton drew a raspy breath as he returned to his seat, his voice shaky as he spoke. "Aye, I suppose I do know. In truth, I've only come for yer assurance that when the murderer is found that ye will do the honorable thing and deliver her to me so that I may punish the lass as I see fit."

"'Twas a lass that killed Lanrick? How? And why? I can think of none in my territory who would do such a thing."

"Aye, 'twas a lass. A bumbling whore of a woman, at that. I wasna there at the time, but Lanrick died from a wound to his head. The lass beat my son to death."

Paton did his best to keep his face expressionless, but surely Laird Morton didn't believe his tale any more than Paton did.

"I need yer assurance that ye will allow my men and me to comb through yer forests and villages, and that ye shall do the same."

"Ye may search the forests as much as ye like, Thayne, but I willna have ye disturbing anyone in their home. I shall, however, spread word so that if the lass is seen, I will be notified of it. If she is found, I will deliver her to ye meself."

"Do ye give me yer word?"

He would feel no guilt for a lie told to a man such as Laird Morton. "Aye, Thayne. I give ye me word."

CHAPTER 16

My head was all the way out the bedroom window when the door to the room opened, and I heard Miren's panicked voice call after me.

"What do ye think ye are doing, lass? Ye canna possibly leave that way."

She rushed over to me, quickly grabbing my arms to pull me back inside. She was right, of course. The distance to the ground was way too far for me to jump, and I doubted my chances of surviving two big falls in one day were very good.

Still, had Miren not stopped me, I might have attempted to at least scale the stone wall of the castle. Even if I fell part of the way down, that was likely to be less painful than whatever Laird Morton intended to do to me if he ever saw me again. I didn't expect I would be given a trial where self-defense would win out. If the old man was anything like his son, the only punishment he would see fit for me was to see my head on a spike.

"Miren, Laird Morton can't know that I'm here. It was his…"

She held up a hand to stop me. "I know, lass. So does Paton. He will make certain that Laird Morton knows nothing about yer presence here at the castle. Now shut the window and get yerself back into bed."

"Are you sure he won't come looking for me?"

Miren shook her head. "In this castle? Nae. Paton willna permit it. I promise ye that ye are safe here. Outside of these walls is where ye will be in danger. Laird Morton willna stop until he finds ye. I'm afraid ye will have to remain within the castle until Paton decides what to do."

"I can't. I have to find my way back home."

She pulled back the covers on the bed and motioned for me to get inside. Ever since finding me, Miren had mothered me, but after really taking in her appearance, I was pretty sure we were quite close in age.

"And where is that, lass? Where is yer home?"

"You can call me Liv, Miren. Lass makes it sound like I'm a child."

She looked slightly offended but gave me a nod as I kicked off my shoes and crawled back into bed. "Verra well. Where is yer home, Liv?"

Miren didn't seem to know about time travel. At least she didn't know about it yet. Paton had promised to explain everything to her in the morning. Would it matter if I went ahead and told her now? I liked the idea of her being in the know. Perhaps it would make her think I was less crazy, and she'd given me no reason so far not to trust her.

"I'm not crazy, Miren. I know I've frightened you some tonight, but I can explain the reason for that, though I'm not certain you'll believe me."

She settled herself onto the edge of the bed, her expression kind. "I ne'er thought ye were crazy. I only thought ye were injured and mayhap confused. Tell me, Liv. I give ye me word that I will listen with an open mind."

"I am not from this time. When I fell off the side of the cliff today, I seemed to have slipped backwards in time."

She stared at me for a long moment before giving me one simple nod. "I do believe ye."

I scrunched up my nose as I regarded her skeptically. "Really? Why?"

"'Tis truly the only thing that explains anything about ye, Liv. Yer clothing, yer speech, Paton's question when he first saw ye. And as for why I believe ye? Ye are no' the first person I've encountered with magic inside ye."

"I don't have magic inside of me. I didn't travel back here on purpose."

Miren shrugged. "Mayhap no', but magic is real, Liv, and ye've been touched by it whether ye possess it or no'."

"What do you mean when you say magic?"

She smiled at me and stood up from the edge of the bed. "'Tis no' me story to tell. Mayhap if ye stay long enough, Paton will tell ye."

"I can't stay here, Miren. I must get back to my sister as quickly as I possibly can."

Miren's expression went blank again, as it often did when I said something that seemed to concern her. It surprised me just how quickly Miren could shift her expressions. One moment she could display tremendous tenderness, the next I wouldn't be able to read her. It seemed to me that she was practiced at hiding her emotions. Even from the brief way she'd mentioned her husband, I suspected she had good reason to do so.

"I know we will all do whatever we can to help ye. Ye might wait just a little to go to sleep, if ye can. I expect Paton will wish to speak to ye again once Laird Morton leaves. Now, if ye promise me that ye willna try to escape through the window again, I might try to get some sleep meself."

Miren had to be nearly as exhausted as I was. I knew I'd given her a fright when they'd found me, and she'd doted on me hand and foot ever since then, and all that was after working a whole day doing whatever it was she did here at the castle.

"I won't be going anywhere tonight, not with Laird Morton so close by. Get some rest, Miren, and thank you so much for everything you've done for me today."

"Aye, Miren. Thank ye."

I looked up to see Paton standing in the doorway, his face concealed in the shadows as he stood just beyond the glow of candlelight.

"Has Laird Morton gone then?"

Paton stepped all the way inside the room, his expression somber and heavy as it became visible in the light.

"Aye. He is gone for now, but the matter itself is far from over. Thayne is set on vengeance."

Miren gave Paton's arm a gentle squeeze as she left the room, and the familiar gesture made me wonder if there was some dynamic between the two of them that I'd missed earlier in the evening. Were they lovers? Good friends? Whatever the case, I knew they had to be more than employer and employee. Even in my own time, I wouldn't have squeezed on my boss like that.

"Another worry for another day. Ye've done all ye can do tonight."

"Aye, lass. Now go and rest. Ye look as if ye've been up for days."

She bid me a quick goodnight as she stepped into the hallway, leaving Paton and me alone.

"Laird Morton wants ye dead, lass. Is Miren right? Did Lanrick intend to rape ye when ye killed him?"

My stomach lurched again, as it did each time memories of that terrifying few minutes flashed through my mind. My emotions surrounding the whole ordeal were mixed in such a way that I had difficulty fully processing any of it. I would never want to be responsible for someone else's death, but I couldn't bring myself to regret it. If I had to do it over, I would've acted no differently.

"Yes, but it wasn't my intention to kill him. I only meant to kick him away from me long enough to have a chance to run away from him. I had no way of knowing that he would land in a way that would crack his head like that."

Paton nodded, as if he'd suspected as much.

"I'll protect ye, lass, but that means ye must stay hidden within this castle for at least the next three moons. I will be unable to get ye off the isle before then."

Three months was unacceptable. Even one night away from Rory would be so traumatic for her that she'd have difficulty recovering from the experience. If I was gone for three months, I'd be dead to her—to my entire family. They would grieve me. There would be a funeral. I'd lose my apartment.

There was no way in hell I could stay in this time for the next three months.

"I can't do that, Paton. I have family whose lives have just been upended. I'll never be able to explain one day of my absence, let alone three months."

Paton sighed and began to pace the room as he spoke to me. "Lass, I truly do wish there was a simple way to see ye home, but I doona know of it. Magic is no' as easily found in Scotland as it once was. Even if 'twas a true portal ye passed through and no' a spell, ye canna verra well try to pass through it again. 'Tis a miracle ye survived the fall once. If 'tis no' a portal, ye would likely kill yerself trying to get back home."

"Wait a minute." I held up a hand to stop him. "You think a spell might've brought me here?"

Paton shrugged and ran a hand over his face as he sighed. I could feel the anxiety rolling off him as he paced.

"I doona know, lass. I've known of only one who cast such spells, and in truth, I dinna know the witch meself."

"Well, can we find her and ask?"

"Nae, lass. She is dead."

Of course she was.

"I believe there may be one other portal, but 'tis located at a castle far, far away from here."

"Well, let's go there, then."

Paton let out a frustrated sigh and moved to sit next to me on the bed, his eyes weary. "'Tis what I am trying to tell ye, lass. I doona wish to hold ye hostage. Laird Morton was already set on destroying me family before the events of this day. Things are even more dire now."

"What do you mean?"

"Me father owed Laird Morton a great deal of money, which he dinna pay back before his death. I have but three months to pay the balance in full. Me only choice is to marry a lass whose family is wealthy enough to see this debt settled. Me first prospect arrives at the castle in a week's time. The trip to and from Castle Cagair would take at least twice that. Laird

Morton's men will be scouring every bit of the forest surrounding this castle and our village. We canna risk trying to leave the isle with ye so soon after Lanrick's death. He intends to put a hefty price on yer head. It willna be only Thayne and his men looking for ye, but many of me own villagers, as well."

While I scarcely knew this man, I could sense his sincerity. He wasn't trying to make my life difficult. It was me who'd just added much difficulty to his. Still, all I could think of was my sister and parents as he tried to explain why we couldn't look for a way to get me back home right away.

"What about my family? They don't know where I've gone. They will grieve me. I can't just do nothing for months knowing that they think I'm dead."

Paton sighed again and allowed his eyes to close as he spoke.

"I will try to think of another solution, lass, but for now, ye must stay hidden here. Believe me, I would ne'er wish grief upon anyone."

I thought I saw a tear form in the corner of his eye, but he stood abruptly before it could fall and left the room without another word.

It wasn't Paton's fault I was here. I couldn't expect him to pause his life for me when he had to save his own family in the months to come, especially when he and everyone else at the castle had already done so much to help me. But he didn't know me very well if he thought I could just sit idly by while he figured something out.

I would try to sleep, and come morning, I would take my chances in the forest. And even if I had to risk throwing myself off that damned cliff again, I owed it to Rory to do everything in my power to try and find the portal that would take me back.

Isle of Skye, Scotland
Present Day

"Lass, if I drive any faster, we shall go tumbling off the edge of this cliffside, as well."

Morna couldn't keep still in her seat. Ages had passed since a spell had gone this wrong. Was she losing her touch? Was age finally catching up with her, weakening her powers? Nothing had gone according to plan with this lass.

The sisters were meant to travel back together. And a fog was supposed to overcome them during their picnic and transport them back. She'd certainly never intended for the poor lass to fall off the edge of a cliff. She could only thank the heavens that she'd seen her mistake in time to cast a spell to keep the lass safe during her fall.

"I am sorry, Jerry. 'Tis only that I must at least provide Olivia's sister with some relief from the trauma I've just put her through. 'Tis the least I can do."

"And how do ye intend to do that?"

"I shall make her forget. No' forever, but until things play out as they are meant to in the past. I can at least give Rory the gift of no' remembering her sister is gone."

CHAPTER 17

Buchannan Castle
17th Century

Sleep didn't come easily to him. All Paton could think of was how much Liv's presence reminded him so much of the lassies he'd known and loved before. He understood the lass' desire to get back home, but he'd make himself a liar if he said he was keen to help her get there. Seeing someone else from the same time as Kate made him feel connected once again to those he'd lost. He could see no reason for her presence here, but whatever strange event had sent the woman hurdling back through time, he was grateful for it. Even if her first day had made his life exceedingly more difficult. He knew Laird Morton well enough to know that vengeance for Lanrick's death—not that he would ever have it—would not be enough for the old bastard. The evil laird would find some way to use his son's death to make their entire territory pay for more than just his father's debt.

There was one within the castle walls who would love their new guest instantly. Paton knew that the moment Ella learned of Lanrick's death, she would worship Liv until the end of her days.

He'd promised Liv he would keep her safe, but he would be unable to do so alone. It would require the efforts and secrecy of every person inside the castle. At least he trusted them all completely.

With the sun just beginning to peek through the window, Paton gave up on sleep and decided it was time to start his day. Miren would already be busy in the castle kitchen, and after retiring so early, he expected his sister would be awake, as well.

They rarely all gathered for breakfast, but today would be the exception. He had much to discuss with them all.

"Do ye have any idea the service this lass has done me, Paton? If Lanrick Morton was the sort of man who would rape someone, what sort of a husband do ye think he would have been?"

Ella's excitement over Lanrick's death, while understandable, made it clear to him how little his sister's faith was in his plan to marry to obtain the funds they needed. Despite his insistence that he would never allow her to marry Lanrick, Paton could tell she'd not really believed it until this very moment.

"I've told ye before, lass. I would ne'er have permitted such a union."

"Aye, but now 'tis certain. Unless Laird Morton knows how to raise someone from the dead."

Bram spoke through a yawn, "I wouldna put it past the man to try. There was murder in his eyes when he left here last night."

Paton agreed. "Aye, which is why I must have the word of everyone here that ye willna speak a word about the lass to anyone in the village. No' even yer husband, Miren."

Her tone was sharp and short as she clipped back at him. "As if I would."

He should've known not to call Miren out in such a way. He knew her better than anyone else gathered around him, save Bram. His assumption wasn't fair to her. He just didn't know her husband, and that's what made him worry.

"Forgive me, lass. I dinna mean to offend ye."

"How do ye intend to keep the lass hidden once the castle is filled to the brim with visitors? If all of Laird McKinsley's family comes, we willna have the rooms for the lass to stay where she is now. And ye canna expect her to ne'er leave her room, sir. I saw how frightened the poor lass was. She doesna deserve to be kept captive here."

Anger flared up inside him at Clara's suggestion. All he was trying to do was protect her.

"O'course she is no' going to be held captive. If the lass has any sense, she shall be pleased to stay put in a room until we can find a way to see her safely off the isle and back home. I know that the timing is poor for all of this, but I see no way around any of it. We must all simply do our best. As for where the lass shall stay, I will think of something. All I need to know is that I have yer word that all of ye will protect her. Laird Morton is a vile man. He son mayhap have been worse."

One by one, everyone promised him their silence.

"Now, let us eat. All of us. Together. Once Laird McKinsely's clan arrives, we will scarcely have time to speak to one another."

Miren stood to head to the kitchen to gather up breakfast and Paton motioned for Davy to help her, but Bram stood up from the table as well.

"I'll help Davy carry the food in. Miren, why doona ye go and wake our guest and invite her down here. If she is to be confined to her room for weeks, the least we can do is give her some freedom within the castle for the next week."

Paton nodded in agreement. He should've thought of it himself.

"Aye, Miren. See the lass down to breakfast."

She left quickly, and when he heard her footsteps coming quickly down the stairs, he grew worried.

"It seems the lass has less sense than ye hoped, Paton. Her room is empty. It seems she's gone."

CHAPTER 18

By the time I found a back door to the castle, I'd made one very important decision about my future once I made it back to my own time. I would never buy any other pair of shoes that weren't sneakers. Had I worn the shoes Miren had given me the night before, my first step outside of the bedroom would've given me away, but my cushy, quiet sneakers allowed me to pad my way through the castle corridors undetected.

I even found a cloak hanging just inside the back door, which I stole without hesitation as I draped it around my shoulders and covered my hair and opened the door as quietly as I could, slipping out into the cool morning air.

Fog draped itself heavily over the castle grounds, weaving its way in and out of the trees. It would be helpful in keeping me hidden, and I was optimistic that I would be able to hear approaching danger from the crackling of branches once I made it all the way into the woods.

It was also still early. Maybe whatever men Laird Morton had scattered throughout the trees would still be sleeping. It was foolish optimism, I knew. Most likely, the day would end up with me dead, but I knew myself well enough to know that I would lose my mind if I did nothing.

It was time for me to at least try to end this nightmare of a trip.

"Where do ye think ye are going, lass? Do ye have a death wish?"

I couldn't see him through the fog. I could only hear his voice. It was close. So close that goosebumps scattered over my flesh.

I froze and sighed as defeat swam over me. For the second time in as many days, I was about to be taken captive.

"Please, Paton. I'll be careful. I have to try."

I heard the crunch of rocks beneath his feet as he moved closer to me, but I could still see nothing around me. Turning, I stepped back until my shoulders touched the castle's stone.

"I know that ye canna begin to understand the dangers that await ye off these grounds, lass, but ye will die if ye leave here. Laird Morton, or some other will find ye. Do ye truly believe he would make quick work of yer death when he does get his hands on ye again? I can assure ye, he would not. Laird Morton has no other children. Ye have killed his only heir. Desperate men will do desperate things. I beg of ye, lass. Come back inside."

Some obstinate, stubborn part of me rebelled against the logic of every word he said. Of course, he knew better what awaited me if I tried this. But still, even against my better judgment, I couldn't bring myself to relent.

"Will you stop me from leaving if I truly wish to?"

There was a long pause, and for a moment I wondered if perhaps he'd gone. Then I heard a frustrated sigh cut through the fog, so close to me I thought I could almost feel his breath against my neck.

"Nae, lass. Ye doona belong to me, and if ye truly willna permit me to help ye, I willna force it upon ye."

I knew I should backtrack on my plan, thank him, and gratefully walk back inside the castle, but some part of me just panicked, and I turned away from him and ran.

I could see nothing, but I felt my feet slip just as I heard Paton yell out to me.

"Ye are going the wrong way, lass. Ye are nearing the edge!"

The ground beneath me shifted as history began to repeat itself and I lost my footing. Only this time, instead of tumbling backwards, I fell onto my butt as the mud beneath me began to slide. I flipped myself around in a scrambled effort to grasp onto something. Just as I braced for another drop, strong hands grabbed at my wrist, and although this stopped my fall, the impact of my body against the rocks caused me to cry out in pain.

I didn't stop wailing as Paton pulled me up and into his arms.

"My ribs! My ribs!"

Everything hurt so much worse than it had the day before, and the fall was so much less.

He held me like a child as he marched confidently away from the cliff edge. How he could see in the fog, I hadn't the slightest idea, but I didn't question his sense of direction.

I could feel how tense he was in his grip, and his breath was ragged and angry as he spoke to me.

"Ye are a damned fool, lass. I have ne'er seen anyone as prone to injure herself in me life."

"I..." I wailed again as I tried to speak. Every breath hurt, and it felt as if he were spinning me in circles. "I think I broke my ribs."

"I wouldna doubt it, though I will take no responsibility for it. Had I no' grabbed ye, ye would've broken more than a few ribs. Ye've just behaved like a stubborn child."

Had I not been in such excruciating pain, I might have argued with him, but in truth, I was also inclined to agree with him. I wasn't some nature-savvy, expert hiker who might have a real shot at getting where I so desperately wanted to go. I was a city girl. One who spent most of my days elbow deep in powdered sugar, not perfecting survival methods.

I didn't try to say anything else, instead allowing my head to fall against his muscular chest as he carried me up the front castle steps, inside, and all the way up to my room without missing a step. He didn't even sound winded—only furious—when he laid me back on the bed.

"Can ye remove yer dress on yer own, or shall I?"

Startled, I took in a raspy breath. "Excuse me?"

"I need to examine yer ribs, lass. No' only that, but yer clothes are soaked through from the fog and drizzle. Do ye wish to rest in a wet bed?"

"Send Miren up here."

"They are searching the castle for ye, lass."

Growing impatient, he reached for me as if he intended to rip the gown right off me.

I held up a hand to stop him. "I'll get it. Go and find Miren and let her look."

He stood, his eyes still filled with fire, "Verra well. Listen, lass, I know that I said I would let ye leave before, but 'tis clear to me now that ye will die if I do so. I must take back what I said. I willna allow ye to leave here until I can escort ye from the castle meself. And as I told ye last night, I canna do that for some time."

My breath was ragged as I shifted in a way that caused pain to shoot through my entire body.

"I don't think I could leave even if I wanted to now."

"Then yer injuries are a blessing, lass. Now, listen to me. I understand yer desperation. I will send Davy to Cagair Castle. Laird Morton willna stop him if he wishes to leave the isle, and he knows his way around Scotland far better than I. He will make the journey and inquire about the portal. At least then ye will have an answer in a matter of weeks, rather than months, aye?"

It was a concession, and after all I'd just put him through, it was the least I could agree to.

"Thank you. I promise I won't try to leave again."

His expression didn't soften as I watched a muscle in his cheek bulge as he spoke through clenched teeth.

"Good. If ye are no' out of that dress by the time I return with Miren, I shall see ye out of it meself. We need to see the extent of yer injuries lass. Do ye understand?"

I nodded, and despite the pain that reverberated up and down my body, some very female part of me urgently wanted to see him follow through with his threat.

CHAPTER 19

Paton's body vibrated with unleashed anger as he stormed through the castle to let everyone know he'd found her. What in the hell was wrong with the lass? Did she wish to die?

He knew his anger to be misplaced, but he couldn't help it. He couldn't bear to see anyone else die.

He bumped into Davy first.

"What's happened? Ye look as if ye mean to strangle me."

He took a deep breath and clenched his fists to try and quelch the surge of adrenaline still coursing through him.

"No' ye, but I canna deny that our dear guest, Olivia, has now just tested my patience."

"So ye found her then."

"Aye, I found her. And I need ye to leave here at once. Do ye know where Cagair Castle is?"

His friend nodded, but his expression showed only

confusion. "Aye, I know of it, though I have ne'er been there. Why?"

"There mayhap be a way to get the lass home there. I doona know if those that were there before still inhabit the place. I believe there should be a man named Orick. If he is still there, he can be trusted. Tell him the lassie's story and see if they still have a way to see the lass back to her own time there."

Davy shook his head and ran his hands through his long hair. "I canna begin to tell ye how much more interesting my life has become since I met ye, Paton. Faeries, time travel, and lassies from the future. It is ne'er boring by yer side."

Paton sighed, the night of no sleep catching up to him. "This moment I long for boring. Will ye go? And doona write. Only a report from yer own lips will do. I doona trust Laird Morton to no' apprehend correspondence once it reaches the isle."

Davy gave him a quick nod and a smile before turning his back toward him.

"O'course I will. Good luck with yer wife hunting. I shall return as soon as I can."

I physically couldn't remove the dress on my own. I'd attempted, but my ribs hurt so much that I ended up just collapsing backwards on the bed while I sobbed. When Paton re-entered the room with Miren by his side, he took one look at me and his expression softened.

Rather than follow through on his threat, he simply nodded in my direction as he addressed Miren.

"Miren, can ye help the lass out of her dress? I shall turn my back to ye both. I assure ye I willna turn back around until her breasts are covered."

I relaxed a little, but even releasing the tension in my muscles hurt terribly.

It took some effort, but eventually Miren was able to shimmy the dress up over my waist so that once the buttons were undone, she could lift it up over my head without me doing much of anything.

Miren gasped when my skin became visible as she pulled the dress off me. I glanced down to see that my skin was already forming deep bruises where my ribs had made impact with the rocks.

"I think it impossible that the lass hasna broken at least a few ribs, Paton."

"Let me see."

He turned toward us quickly, and I had to jerk to cover my breasts with the blanket in front of me. His eyes widened as he looked me over.

"You look surprised, Paton."

"I am. I had hoped that ye only had a female's normal low tolerance for pain."

Miren and I both shot daggers in his direction with our eyes.

"Are you fucking joking?"

He reared back in surprise. "Aye, I was, lass. Though I can see by the way the hairs on my back have just risen in fear from the expression on both yer faces that mayhap was no' the proper time. Ye've a colorful command of language, Liv."

I glared at him as he continued to stare down at my bruised and swollen skin.

"If you felt the way I do right this second, I daresay that your language might be a little more colorful than normal, too."

"We must have the healer brought to the castle again straight away."

I groaned as I laid back down and covered my skin up more fully.

"I doubt there is much she can do. They will just take time to heal."

"She should at least be able to give ye something for the pain." He turned away from me, and I allowed my eyes to close as I listened to the instructions he gave Miren.

"I've sent Davy away, but I shall have Bram and Clara go down into the village to fetch her."

"Let Clara stay here. If ye will permit it, I truly do need to go home for the day to check on Murray. He is no' well himself, and I have been away for too long."

"Verra well. Bram will see ye into town. He can return with the healer."

My eyes shot open when I felt his hand touch my cheek.

"We will see ye feeling better as soon as we can, lass."

With that, he turned and left me yearning for the touch of his hands. For that brief second, I'd forgotten all about my pain. All I'd been able to feel was the warmth of his fingers against my skin. Perhaps it was my brain trying to distract me from the pain, but I couldn't help but wonder just how lovely it would be to have those strong hands touch me elsewhere.

CHAPTER 20

"How are ye, Bram?"

For most of the ride into the village, they'd been silent, both unwilling to speak of anything involving Olivia that might be heard by Laird Morton or his men. But Miren knew the old man wouldn't care about this, and she truly did wish to know the answer.

For a time in her life, when she and Paton were childhood sweethearts, she and Bram had been the dearest of friends. She couldn't pinpoint exactly when things changed between them, when the contact became less frequent, and eventually their lives spun them off in different directions, but she'd always liked him. She always would. And her heart had ached for him ever since the moment she'd learned of Lady Winnifred's death.

"I am well enough, though I am no' so accustomed to waking so early."

"I think ye know that is no' what I meant. She's been gone

for some time now. I suppose many have stopped asking ye, stopped checking in. Truly, how are ye?"

Miren turned her attention back to the road in front of them, hoping that Bram might speak more freely without her gaze focused right at him. It took him a moment, but eventually, he answered her.

"They say time heals all things, though I am no' so sure 'tis true. I can pull meself from bed now and can get through the day without drinking meself into a stupor, but there is a constant ache," Miren looked at him as he paused and tapped the center of his chest, "right in me center that makes me feel as if I might crumble to dust any moment."

Instinctively, she reached for his hand, squeezing it. "She was a lucky lass. I only saw her once, the day she came to the village to see the dressmaker. I was there to pick up some fabric and couldna help but hear the way she spoke of ye. She adored ye, Bram. Ye made her verra happy."

She kept hold of his hand as a sob escaped him, as she reached for the reins to give him a moment.

"I am sorry, Miren. I shouldna cry in front of ye."

She patted the top of his hand, dismissively. "Nonsense. There is no better person ye could cry in front of."

"Sometimes I feel as if I am the only one left who loved her. Her parents fled the isle after her death, and I doubt I shall ever see them again. I'll ne'er be able to swap stories about her with them, ne'er be able to look into her mother's face and see the familiar smile I loved so verra much."

"The past few years have been too much for ye, Bram. Ye are stronger than I e'er think I shall be."

Bram lifted her hand then, and she could sense his desire to brush away his sadness as his expression shifted, and she watched as he spotted the bruise on her wrist.

"And ye are stronger than any should have to be. Where did ye get this bruise?"

Bram suspected the truth—everyone did—but she couldn't very well tell him that what he could see on her wrist was nothing compared to Murray's usual handiwork.

Miren snatched her hand away from Bram's grip. "I lost my footing when Davy and I were helping Olivia into the castle. I hit it on one of the stone steps."

She turned away from his disbelieving gaze as they neared the edge of the village.

"Why did ye marry him, Miren?"

She was loath to admit it. She found it difficult to reconcile the naïve, frightened young girl she'd been with the woman she was today.

"The truth?"

"Always."

"Because he asked me. When yer brother left, no one else would. I think everyone thought Paton would return some day and none wanted to be the lad that took Paton Buchannan's lass away from him. Murray was the only man who dinna care about that."

Bram let out a gruff, throaty noise. "Did ye ever think there might be reason for that, lass?"

Some part of her bristled at his question. Who was he to question her judgment, even if she did admittedly question her own? Bram Buchannan was a man, one born of more privilege than most. He would never understand what drove any woman to the decisions that so many were forced to make to get by in a world not built for them.

"O'course, I did, but what else was I supposed to do, Bram? If I wanted a place in the village, if I dinna wish to be shunned for being an old maid, I had to marry, and none save Murray asked."

"I have never liked him." Bram's tone remained judgmental and disapproving.

She didn't like him either. Not anymore. But what other choice did she have but to lie in the bed she made.

"'Tis a good thing he dinna ask for yer hand then, aye? I am close enough to home now. Let me out and I shall walk the rest of the way. I doona want Murray to see ye through the window. Ye know the way to the healer's house."

He reached out for her hand, but she was already making her jump onto the ground.

"Miren, lass. I dinna mean to offend ye. 'Tis only I worry for ye."

She whirled toward him as she backed away from the horses. "Ye needn't Bram. I can manage on me own. I have done so for a verra long time now. I'll see ye come morning. Please wait for me here, and I shall meet ye."

CHAPTER 21

Paton tried to busy himself around the castle, but he only grew more anxious with each moment that passed without Bram's swift return to the castle. Olivia needed pain relief. He could hear her raspy, pained breaths each time he paused outside of her bedchamber. He should've been back long ago.

"Will you just please come inside here and keep me company?"

Paton jumped at the unexpected sound of her voice before guiltily peeking his head in through the door.

"I wasna just standing here, lass. I only meant to see if ye were sleeping."

She struggled to lift her hand to wave him inside. "I know, but I'm not. I'm hurting too badly to sleep, and I'm losing my mind just lying here. Clara said she had too much to do to visit with me, and the older man, what's his name?"

"Chambers."

"Oh yeah. Chambers acted as if my suggestion that he stay and visit with me were the most scandalous proposal he'd ever heard in his life."

He laughed and moved to sit in the chair still positioned by her bed. "I canna say I blame him, lass. Ye are naked."

Her cheeks flushed slightly, but she recovered quickly. She even gave him a gentle smile as he settled in for their chat.

"He couldn't see anything. But it's no matter. I expect you'll provide the most interesting conversation anyway."

"Ye are mistaken, lass. Me sister would entertain ye far more, but I shall do me best. I must confess, I am surprised ye have no' seen her. She's been eager to meet the lass she believes saved her life."

"Oh, I believe she tried to come and see me. I did hear Clara reprimand someone out in the hall. She gave whoever it was strict instructions to stay away. Part of me wondered if it was you, and that's why you were lingering outside my door without entering."

It was his turn to blush. She'd not believed him when he said he was checking to see if she slept. In truth, he'd spent all day trying to resist the temptation to stay right by her side.

"Och, nae, 'twasna me. In a while, I shall have to go and find me sister. Ye will like her."

"I'm sure I will. Why does she believe I saved her life?"

"The debt to Laird Morton I told ye of. Under our original agreement, she was set to marry Lanrick Morton if I dinna come up with the funds. Now that ye've killed him, even if I fail, my sister will at least avoid that terrible fate."

"Oh." Her expression gave away everything her words did not. She didn't approve of the arrangement.

"'Tis no' I who agreed to the betrothal, lass. While I still find it difficult to believe, 'twas my late father's agreement with Laird Morton."

Her expression relaxed a little.

"Good. While I can't find it within me to say that I'm glad I killed him, I'm not sorry that Lanrick Morton is unable to hurt anyone else. I'm sure I wasn't the first, nor would I have been the last."

"Aye, lass. Ye are right, I am certain."

A beam of sunlight caught on something as the light outside shifted, and Paton squinted his eyes to make it out. A cobweb—a large one glistened in the sun. Paton stood and walked over toward the window to brush it away, only to find others.

As he took in the room for the first time, guilt settled inside him. The room was unsuited to guests. Cobwebs and dust littered the small, cold room. They had much to do to ready the castle before Laird McKinsley's arrival.

He turned back toward Liv as he made his decision.

"We are moving ye, lass. Ye will no' spend another night in this dreadful room."

She shook her head at him dismissively. "It's fine. Truly. Just a little bit of dust here and there."

"'Tis dreadful, lass, and I am sorry that I dinna notice the state of it sooner. Me only defense is that ye have directed our attentions elsewhere since the moment ye arrived."

"I'm not sure I can actually bring myself to walk down the hall, if I'm honest."

"I've carried ye before, Liv. I've no reason to believe that I canna do it again."

"I'm naked, remember?"

Somehow, he hadn't, but her reminder caused a bolt of need to shoot through him, making him hard. Thank God for the thickness of his kilt. Ages had passed since such a longing had stirred within him. Not that there was anything he could do about it now. The lass was far too injured to feel any such need herself.

"I shall send Clara up to assist ye while I ready me own bedchamber."

Her voice went up a full octave when she responded to him. "Your bedchamber? Where will you sleep?"

Had she truly thought he would bring her to his room with plans to stay there himself?

"In here, lass. I intend to switch places with ye. At least until we see this room returned to a state of cleanliness."

"I really am fine."

He was already on his way out the door.

"Nonsense, lass. 'Tis the only bedchamber ye've seen in the castle. Once ye see me own, ye will see how no' fine ye truly were in here."

The actual act of Paton lifting me from the bed and into his arms was painful enough to make the room spin around me, but once settled against his chest, I was quite sure the momentary pain was worth it.

Where was the tall, strapping man to carry me around my apartment back home?

The castle hallways were long and winding, so I had plenty of time to enjoy the feeling of his muscles pressed against my face as he held me tight against him.

The man was abnormally good looking, and the more time I spent with him, the more I realized that he was also abnormally kind. He was the sort of man that if I'd met him in my own time —if men such as this even existed then—I'd be in trouble.

When we did finally reach Paton's room and we stepped inside, my jaw visibly went slack from shock. It was the most exquisite and large bedroom I'd ever seen. Furs lay across the cold stone floors, and a fire taller than me roared in the massive fireplace in front of several beautiful wooden chairs in the corner. The bed was at least twice the size of the one I'd been in before, and the luscious look of it had me dying to get inside.

"Wow."

"'Tis better, aye? No' a cobweb to be found in here, lass."

"It's beautiful."

"'Twas my parents' place of refuge for one another when they were alive. I have tried to honor their love of this room while also making it me own."

He carried me over to the bed and laid me back into a mattress that rivaled any I'd slept on in my own time.

"I am so verra sorry for Bram's delay, lass. I can only assume the healer must be with someone else in the village whose need is greater. I know ye are in need of relief from yer pain. Would ye take a drink, lass? 'Twould help, I am certain."

I would've let him shoot me with a horse tranquilizer if he thought it would help with the pain. And had I known there was alcohol readily available, I would've gotten myself good and toasted hours ago. Anything to numb me from the constant throbbing.

"I would love one. The stronger, the better."

Paton laughed and walked across the room. "We shall see about that, lass. I doona expect ye will be accustomed to drink as stout as this."

When he brought me the dram and extended the amber

liquid toward me, the smell alone was enough to tell me he was right.

"Bottoms up." I smiled as I threw back the drink, and nearly immediately threw it back up at him. The only thing that stopped me was the pain such a motion would cause my ribs.

Paton began to laugh. "I did warn ye."

I coughed as the liquid continued to burn its way down my throat. "That's not alcohol. That's fire starter."

"Would ye like another?"

I couldn't very well allow my survival of the first drink to be for nothing. I was at least going to get some pain relief out of it.

"I'd like two."

Paton laughed every step as he walked back across the room to pour me more of the heinous drink.

CHAPTER 22

"Bram Buchannan, what brings ye into the village?"

Bram pulled hard on his horse's reins at the sound of Laird Morton's voice behind him, turning his horse toward the sound. He couldn't risk Laird Morton seeing him go to the healer. The man would ask too many questions, and none of them could risk having him come to the castle once again.

He smiled and did his best to keep his expression warm as he answered him.

"I was seeing the lass we have cooking for us back to her home for the night. I intended to seek ye out, as well, to inquire if anyone caught sight of the lass you are looking for today."

Laird Morton was drunk. The old man could scarcely keep his eyes open as he staggered out the doors of the tavern. Perhaps, he could get the man even more so. Passed out would be best, then Bram could go about his business.

He dismounted quickly and led his horse toward the others as Thayne answered him.

"Nae. The lass has no' been seen. It seems like yer chef, she has vanished. But we will keep up the search."

"Should ye no' go home, Thayne? Do ye no' need to be with yer wife during this difficult time for ye and yer family?"

"That bitch ne'er cared for Lanrick as I did. She no more needs me there to grieve with than I do her."

Bram stepped around Laird Morton and opened the door to the tavern as he ushered the man inside.

"Let me get ye another drink then. Ye look as if ye are in need of it."

The man could hold his drink. It took twice as long and three times as many drinks as it would have taken him to pass out before Laird Morton slumped over in his chair snoring. But when he stepped into the cold night air, his heart sank. Since entering the tavern with the old man, his men had since left the forest and gathered in the village for the evening. He would be unable to bring the healer back to the castle without being seen.

Frustrated, Bram gathered his horse and led the creature by hand as he walked through the sleepy village. Just on the edge of town lay Miren's home. He couldn't say why, but something inside drew him nearer to the small, meager cottage.

She was still up. He could see candlelight through the windows. There was no reason for him to continue his approach, but his feet seemed to move despite himself. As he grew nearer, his stomach grew tight with rage.

The bastard was screaming at her. He could hear the man's deep, bellowing voice from a good distance away. What he said, Bram couldn't quite make out, but there was no way he could make himself leave now without ensuring that Miren was safe.

As he neared, he could finally make out the cruel man's words.

"Have ye made yerself a whore then? 'Tis clear that ye have. Why else would ye stay there overnight?"

Miren's voice was barely audible, and there was a fear in her tone he'd never heard before when she spoke.

"Murray, yer anger is senseless. 'Twas the maid, Clara. The old lass fell ill, and they needed me help to care for her. Ye know that I would never be unfaithful to ye."

Murray's voice grew louder as Bram made his way to the door and quietly pressed his ear in close.

"Ye dare say me anger is senseless when I've a whore for a wife?"

Miren screamed then, and Bram could stay outside no longer. With one swift kick, he smashed the door open and stepped inside to see Miren standing next to her husband's bed, her face twisted in pain as her husband bent her wrist behind her back.

"If ye wish to live past this night, ye shall unhand yer wife at once."

Murray smiled at him, a sickly grin that only served to make Bram more resolute in what he knew he had to do.

"Ye dare to come into me home and tell me what I must do with me wife? Are ye the man me wife has been playing the whore with?"

Bram withdrew his sword and in two quick strides he stood next to the bed as he glared down at Murray. Slowly, he brought his sword to the man's neck and pressed it up against Murray's skin.

"Let her go, Murray."

The man maintained his grip on Miren's wrist.

"Do ye mean to kill me, then? Ye willna do it, lad. Ye are no' the killing kind."

His grip on his sword tightened as he narrowed his eyes and pressed it into the man more deeply.

"I wouldna be so sure. Unhand yer wife. She is leaving with me this night and will reside at the castle from here on."

He glanced over at Miren to gauge her expression. All he could see there was relief. He pressed on.

"Ye will ne'er see yer wife again. Once word of yer deeds has spread through the village, which I assure ye they shall, ye will have no place here on this isle."

Still smiling, Murray tightened his grip on Miren's wrist.

"Ye canna steal a man's wife, lad. She is me property. Besides, none will believe her."

"They doona need to believe her. They only need to believe me, and I can assure ye they shall. None like ye, Murray. Ye've far more enemies than friends. Ye must realize there is naught ye can do to stop me. I'll only say it once more. Release the lass or I shall drive this blade through your throat. And I shall promise ye this: no matter how this night may end, whether ye keep yer life or no', ye will ne'er hurt nor see Lady Miren again."

For the first time, Murray released Miren. She quickly ran to the other side of the room and began to collect some of her belongings in a small satchel. With Miren now free, Bram lowered his sword.

It took only seconds for Murray's sickening smile to return. "I knew ye wouldna kill me, lad."

Once more Bram raised his sword. "Mayhap no'. Killing ye would be too easy. But I shall ensure that ye ne'er harm any other lass with at least this hand."

With one great swing, the blade came slicing down, right through Murray's hand; it rolled onto the floor as the miserable man began to scream.

CHAPTER 23

The lass must've been more booze than woman by this point in the evening, but by God the lass was a bonny drunk. At least she no longer complained of her ribs as she lay in bed while they talked late into the night.

He'd refrained from drinking himself. The lass needed the numbing, and all such drinking would do to him is make him want to kiss the lass more than he already did. But all of that would have to wait for another time. Olivia was much too far into the bottle for him to dream of kissing her while she was in such a state.

"Are ye no' weary yet, lass? I should think this much drink would've made ye sleepy much faster."

She smiled at him, her cheeks rosy and her eyes glassy.

"You would think that I would be, but ya know, I'm really not."

Paton smiled and patted her feet beneath the blankets. At some point in the evening, he'd moved from his seat in the chair beside her and now sat across from her at the end of the bed.

"Kick yer feet out from under the blankets, lass, and I shall rub them. Mayhap 'twill soothe ye enough to help ye sleep. Ye do need to sleep. 'Tis when yer body will be most able to heal itself."

She didn't hesitate to do exactly what he asked, though she shivered as soon as her feet were exposed to air.

"I'm never going to turn down a massage. Hurry up and get to rubbing. It's freezing in here.

The fire had long since died, and only a few candles remained flickering in the room around them as he took one of her delicate, smooth feet between his calloused and rough hands and began to rub it.

In truth, while he'd enjoyed his evening with her more than any he could remember in his life, his desire for her to sleep was born out of pure necessity of the weariness that was quickly dragging him toward sleep himself.

The past days had been long and stressful, and he'd slept little the night before.

He concentrated on the massage, firmly pressing his thumb into her tight and tired muscles, and slowly the lass began to drift. And while he'd truly intended to leave her, his eyes began to close, and together, she under the blankets and him on top near her feet, they let sleep finally take them.

Miren screamed as she watched her husband's severed hand land on the floor with a thud, and in that instance, she knew her nightmare was finally over.

Tears sprang to her eyes as she reached for her mother's portrait and several of her dresses and shoved them deep into her only satchel.

Murray could have the rest—if he survived the wound Bram had just given him. She wanted nothing else to remind her of the life she'd had there. She didn't care if she would be outcast for leaving him or that she would never be able to marry again. Something had been different in Murray's eyes tonight as he grabbed her. He was as done as she. While he might not have planned to murder her this night, the day was coming when she knew that he would.

Bram had saved her life, and she would live happily with whatever the consequences of his actions were.

She couldn't bring herself to look at Murray as Bram ushered her into the cold night air. It was only when his arms came around her that she realized how violently she was shaking.

"Come lass. Ye are done with this place. Ne'er again will ye have to sleep in fear."

Sobs broke free, and her knees weakened as she sunk into Bram's supportive embrace in the cold evening air.

"Should I send for Nina, lass, or do we leave his wound to fate?"

"He always told me that a woman's screams meant naught. Mayhap now he will see if a man's screams are worth more than mine. Someone will come. Let them be the judge of his character."

Murray's screams pierced through the night sky, and sure enough, it wasn't long before footsteps from the nearest cottage could be heard rushing toward them.

"Go and stand near me horse, Miren. Doona come near while I speak to yer neighbors."

"What do ye mean to tell them?"

"The truth, lass. Every bit of it. Then they can decide whether or no' the man lying in that bed is worth saving."

It took no time for Bram's conversation to end, and much to Miren's disappointment, the couple rushed inside their home. Murray would likely live to see another day, but at least she could rest easy knowing that she would no longer be in his life. Bram would protect her. She'd never been more certain of anything.

When he returned to her, he helped her mount his horse then deftly climbed up behind her as he pulled her in close and they began their ride back to her new home.

"Are ye angry with me, lass? Ye spoke defensively of him earlier this day, but when I heard what he said to ye, and then I heard ye scream, I couldna stay on the other side of that door."

"Och, Bram. O'course I'm no' angry with ye. Do ye know how many times I've screamed in that home? Enough times to know that ye canna be the first one to hear me. But ye are the only one who cared enough to come inside. Ye saved me life today, and I shall love ye forever for it."

She thought she heard his breath catch in his throat, but he said nothing else. Instead, she felt his lips gently brush against the back of her hair.

For the first time since she was a young girl, Miren felt something inside her she suspected might be hope.

CHAPTER 24

I couldn't be sure how long I'd slept. I hardly remembered falling asleep at all, but when I opened my eyes to see candles still burning but no sunlight streaming in, I knew it was still nighttime.

Even the effort of opening my eyes was painful, and I knew that all my drinking session had done was add to my pain. Sure, it had dulled the pain in my ribs for a time, or at least lessened my ability to focus on it. But now, slightly more sober and already feeling hungover, the rib pain was back with a vengeance. My head felt like someone had just thrown an axe right between my eyes. Not only that, but I needed to pee so badly that my legs were shaking.

I lay there trying to talk myself into getting into a sitting position when I heard someone else's breath near me, a soft snoring sound that caused me to freeze in panic. I reached over with my right hand to find the space beside me empty. Then memories of a few hours earlier came crashing in.

Paton.

I breathed a sigh of relief as I stretched out my toes to feel for him. Sure enough, there he was, passed out cold at the end of the bed.

Then, I realized that I was no longer in the room I was familiar with, and I had no idea where his chamber pot was. To make matters worse, I'd somehow not urinated once since injuring my ribs. I wasn't sure that I could squat down that far on my own.

Resigning myself to the humiliation I knew I was about to face, I nudged Paton with my foot as I called out to him.

"Paton…Paton, I need you to wake up."

The only response I received was an even louder snore.

This time I prodded him with a little more force and raised my voice a little.

"Paton, wake up. I need you."

He let out one loud snort as he woke, and I couldn't help but smile as I watched him jump into a sitting position, his hair mussed in the sexiest way. While he'd not had anything to drink the night before, I suspected he would be as disoriented as I was to see that we'd fallen asleep in bed together.

"Olivia, lass, what troubles ye? I…I must apologize to ye. I give ye me word that I dinna mean to fall asleep in here."

If he hadn't, I had no idea what I would've done. Besides the fact that I didn't imagine any woman would bemoan the likes of a man like him in their bed, I needed him here with me for what was about to have to happen.

"You don't need to apologize. I'm glad you're here."

He looked pleased, and his dimple appeared as he grinned. "Ye are?"

"Yes, I need your help."

He looked at me mischievously. "I'll no' be getting ye another drink, lass. Ye've had more than yer fill."

Even the mention of anything liquid made my need even more urgent.

"No. I don't want a drink. Paton, I need to pee. Like right this second."

His expression changed, and I could see him play through the logistics just as I had. He knew how badly I was hurt. I was also quite sure he knew the position I would have to get in to pee.

"Are ye still numb, lass?"

I shook my head. "Nope. I can barely raise myself up in the bed."

He nodded. His expression serious and resigned. "Verra well. I shall help ye, and then we shall ne'er speak of this again."

I frowned, knowing that this was sure to be the death nail in any sexual tension that might ever occur between the two of us. Really though, who was I kidding? Of course, this man wouldn't have been interested anyway, but that hadn't stopped me from dreaming about it since the first moment I laid eyes on him.

"Is Miren back?"

He frowned at me. "I doona believe so, and she and Bram's absence worries me greatly."

"Clara?"

Again he shook his head. "The lass is old enough to be me grandmother, and she worked herself ragged around the castle today. I willna be waking her for this when I am more than capable of helping ye. 'Tis a natural enough act, lass. We will both survive it."

I really wasn't sure that we would. "What about your sister? I haven't met her yet."

He laughed at me as he rose from the bed and walked across the room to grab the chamber pot. "And this is how ye wish me to introduce her to ye? Besides lass, she is no' tall nor strong enough to help ye hold yerself up."

I groaned as I nodded. "Okay. We will never speak of this again, right? You promise?"

He smiled at me and moved to lift me from the bed. "Aye, lass. I can assure ye I willna wish to remember this any more than ye shall."

That statement made me feel exactly zero percent better.

While I was able to hobble over to the chamber pot, the act of spreading my legs out on either side of it nearly dropped me to the floor. Paton stepped in immediately and placed his arms underneath my arm pits to hold me steady.

"I shallna look at a thing, lass. Hike up yer dress, and I shall hold ye steady as ye take care of yer business."

I attempted to do as he asked but couldn't reach down far enough to grab my dress. Something between a sob and a laugh escaped me as I dropped my head and sighed. I felt like a rag doll as he held me up.

"I…I can't grab it."

He picked me up enough so that my legs were no longer spread around the pot, and I could stand upright on my own again.

"I shall have to bend down and gather yer dress up for ye before we spread ye over the opening, lass."

I shook my head. "You'll see my butt."

"It canna be more offensive than the bruises I saw on ye

earlier, but I give ye me word that I will keep me eyes closed until I am standing and willna peek at ye."

The last thing I wanted to do was to flash him, but my bursting bladder won out over my pride.

"Fine."

I closed my own eyes as he went about his business. Once the bottom half of me was bare, he resumed his position and lifted me over the opening as I found immediate relief.

I was mid-stream, my open legs and bush facing the door when it burst open and Bram came rushing inside.

His jaw fell open, and he hurriedly covered his eyes. I nearly fainted from embarrassment.

"Forgive me. I should've knocked. 'Tis only that I…I dinna expect the lass to be in yer bedchamber brother. Something has happened that I must tell ye right away."

To his credit, Paton kept his grip on me and kept his voice steady as he answered his brother.

"I shall be out shortly. Now, for the love of God, give us some privacy."

Hiding in a bedchamber for the next three months was sure to be no problem. I would never be able to show my face to anyone else in the castle ever again anyway.

CHAPTER 25

Paton knew his cheeks were red as he joined his brother in the sitting room. The moment Bram heard him approach, his brother spun toward him.

"Do I even wish to know what the two of ye were doing?"

Paton kept his face stern as he answered him. "I think ye saw full well what we were doing. The lass needed to relieve herself, and she needed assistance because someone ne'er returned with the healer who could relieve her of her pain."

Bram's expression shifted. "Aye, I know, and I'm sorry for it, but there was no way for me to do so. Laird Morton has men camped all over the village. I couldna risk them telling Thayne that we brought her here. He would wish to know why, and we've no good reason to tell him."

Bram was right, and the irritation he'd been harboring all evening toward his brother vanished.

"Ye were right to do so, but we must find a way to see her

here on the morrow. We canna keep Liv drunk for the entirety of her injury. She might go blind from it."

Bram chuckled. "I can think of worse ways to lose one's sight. Though aye, o'course we must get the lass more aid on the morrow. In the meantime, I've something to tell ye. Before I do, ye must know that I've already given the lass me word. I know ye are laird here, but in this matter, ye must allow me choice to be law. Aye?"

Paton raised his brows in curiosity. "What lass are ye speaking of, lad? And what did ye tell her?"

"Miren, Paton. She has left her husband, and I have assured her that she can find a permanent home here at the castle."

Paton didn't hesitate. Whatever the reason for the events that led to this decision, he would support it if it got Miren out of any situation that caused her harm.

"O'course the lass has a home here. She has always been family to us. What happened?"

Paton listened in both horror and awe as Bram walked him through all that had happened. When he was finally done, Paton reached over to clasp the man on the back.

"I would've done the same, brother. While Murray Black may yet try to cause us trouble if he ever heals from his injuries, we will together ensure that Miren is free from harm from this day forward. Now, why doona the two of us find solace and sleep knowing that we both did good deeds this day."

Once Bram was gone, Paton remained in the sitting room. How he ached to return to his bedchamber, to crawl beneath the covers and wrap his arms around the lass that had made him laugh so much over the course of the evening that his muscles would be sore from it tomorrow. But he could not. He would not.

Instead, he took a seat by the fire and tried to get comfortable enough to sleep.

The first time he'd slept with Olivia had been an accident. The second time would be at her bidding.

Somehow, despite my humiliation, I was able to go to sleep after Paton helped me back into bed, but my dreams were weird and disjointed.

I wasn't even sure I was sleeping, but I knew that I had to be when I couldn't move in the dream. I lay there paralyzed as I lay in Paton's bed, gazing around the room as candles flickered around me.

A soft knock at the bedroom door drew my attention, but when I opened my mouth to speak to whoever was on the other side, no noise would come out.

Slowly, the door creaked open and inside stepped a woman I'd not thought twice about since meeting her—Morna, the kind elderly woman from the hotel restaurant my first night in Scotland.

She smiled at me, but I found myself unable to do the same as she approached.

"Doona worry, lass. I willna hurt ye."

I wasn't frightened, exactly, but I found everything about the situation unnerving-the fact that I could not move or smile or speak, the fact that a woman I hardly knew was someone showing up in my dream in Paton's bedroom.

"I want ye to know that I dinna intend for yer journey to be as difficult as it was. I mean to make it up for ye in some small way. First, ye must know that yer sister is well, lass. I thought that mayhap put yer mind at ease. Second, I will leave ye with this."

The old woman bent and gently rubbed both of her thumbs over my brows before leaning in to kiss the top of my forehead. A warmth rushed through my body. When I looked up she was gone and my dream faded to black.

And when I woke up in the morning, to my everlasting wonderment, all of the pain in my ribs, all of the bruising, even the hangover which I wholly deserved, had vanished.

CHAPTER 26

"So, I may meet her today?"

Paton smiled at Ella as he popped another bite of breakfast into his mouth. "Aye. Clara was overly hasty to keep ye away from the lass yesterday. I am certain she would've enjoyed yer company."

"Can I bring breakfast to her, then?"

Paton hesitated. "The lass is no longer in the room she was in yesterday. Perhaps, 'tis best if I bring breakfast to her today."

Ella frowned. "Where is she, then?"

"In me room."

His sister's eyes widened in disapproval. "Paton! The poor lass has only been here for two nights, she's injured, and yet still ye sought to bring her to yer bed."

"Ella, I doona think this conversation proper."

She scoffed at him. "'Tis yer behavior that isna proper, brother. And doona act surprised that I know of such things. If

I'm old enough to be wed, then I'm old enough to know about the ways between men and women."

"I dinna sleep with her, Ella. I slept in the sitting room and me neck has paid the price for me selflessness this morning. I only moved her to me room because the room she was in wasna fit for a dog to sleep in."

He knew he exaggerated. There were many in the village that would give their last coin to spend one night in the most meager of rooms inside the castle, but any room featuring cobwebs as its artwork wasn't suited for any lass as fine and lovely as Liv.

"Well then, I canna see why I shouldna be able to bring the lass breakfast. She must be hungry."

"Aye, I'm sure she is. Ye must forgive her though if her mood isna as bright as it might otherwise be. She is in much pain, and if I were to wager on it, I'd say 'tis no' only her ribs which are aching her this morning. But aye, ye may bring her breakfast. I shall accompany ye to make the introduction."

"I'm actually feeling much better."

Paton stood abruptly from the sound of Liv's voice in the doorway.

"Did Miren come and help ye dress, lass? I am surprised she managed to help ye down the stairs on her own."

As she approached, Paton took in the sight of her, his eyes wide and confused. She walked straight and tall, her breathing didn't catch uncomfortably, the color of her cheeks was healthy, and her brows were no longer furrowed in pain.

"I truly can't explain it, but I seem to have healed overnight."

Paton stared blankly at her as his mind struggled to make sense of how such an event could have occurred. Was the lass herself magic, and she didn't know it? Were his own powers somehow coming back? He'd certainly wanted to heal her. Had he somehow done so? No. Magic was something he'd been able to feel within him when he possessed it. He could feel no such presence now.

Ella stood, as well, and moved across the room to greet her, but Paton moved quickly and cut his sister off as he reached for Olivia's arm and walked her from the room.

"What are you doing? Your sister is going to think I'm so rude. She was just about to say hello."

He kept his grip on her wrist as she walked along beside him, back up the stairs and toward his bedchamber. He needed answers right away. If there was magic within the lass, then perhaps a great many of their problems could be solved more easily than he'd imagined possible.

"She willna think ye rude. She will think I am. She'll be fine. Ye can speak to her later. I must…I must speak with ye."

If I needed further evidence of my full and complete miraculous recovery, I received confirmation as I was able to keep up with Paton's frantic pace as he moved through the castle without dropping to my knees in pain.

When we finally made it back inside his room, he shut the door and whirled toward me, stepping forward until my back pressed flush against the door.

"Have ye ever seen evidence of yer powers before, lass?"

"Huh?"

"In other times in yer life, have instances of magic happened around ye? Things ye couldna explain. If ye sit quietly with yerself, do ye ever feel a humming, a small vibration within ye?"

I stared at him blankly. "You mean before I fell off a cliff and ended up hundreds of years in the past? No. I can assure you that I have never felt nor witnessed any evidence of magic, or whatever this is, before now."

"Do ye feel something within ye now?"

I did feel something, but only if desire was somehow magic. When he stood that close to me, I could feel my skin flush red as my temperature spiked and my breath came just a little more quickly. All I wanted to do was launch myself at him.

Instead, I shook my head and placed a hand on his chest to back him up as I stepped away from the door.

"No, Paton. I am quite sure that I don't have magical powers."

"Ye must. Ye traveled back in time in a way I've never seen before, and ye now have healed yerself of injuries that most would take months to heal from. 'Tis the only explanation."

While it made no sense, I knew there was another explanation that had to be true.

"Actually, I think someone healed me in my sleep last night."

"Did someone enter this room, lass, after I left ye?"

"No. But someone came to me in a dream."

He continued to pepper me with questions.

"Do ye know who 'twas? Describe them to me. What did they do to ye? Are ye certain 'twas a dream?"

It seemed ridiculous. I didn't even want to tell him, but there was no denying that I'd gone to sleep in extraordinary pain, and after my dream, woke up with none. As strange as the past few days had been, I assumed that it wasn't all that ridiculous to believe that this could be real too.

"It's the strangest thing. I met this woman our first night in Scotland, when we were still in our own time. She was just a sweet, old lady on a weekend trip with her husband. I visited with her for maybe fifteen minutes, tops. I've not thought of her since then. I saw her in my dream. She came inside the room, told me my sister was okay, apologized for what had happened to me, and then kissed my forehead. That was it. Then, I woke up."

Paton's expression shifted, and he hesitated before he asked his next question.

"Do ye...do ye remember the lass' name?"

"I do. Her name was Morna."

Paton closed his eyes and began to shake his head back in forth, as he murmured to himself and began to pace around the room.

"'Tis no' possible."

"Are you okay?"

He stopped midstride and glanced over at me, his eyes angry and disbelieving.

"Ye are mistaken, lass. 'Tis no' the name of the woman ye met or saw in yer dream."

I didn't understand the shift in his tone or how I'd upset him so quickly.

"I truly don't think I am. Her name was Morna, and her husband's name," I hesitated as I tried to remember, "was Jordan." I knew as soon as I said it that didn't sound right. "No. It wasn't Jordan. It was Jerry. Their names were Morna and Jerry."

He narrowed his eyes at me, and his tone was tight and sorrowful as he spoke. "Nae, lass. Morna and Jerry are dead. I saw their bodies myself."

He all but ran from the room, slamming the door behind him as I was left to contemplate what in the hell he was talking about.

CHAPTER 27

He needed air. Needed the frigid morning breeze to fill up his lungs and calm him as his mind spun with the impossibility of what Olivia had just told him.

The lass couldn't have known that he knew of the witch. She didn't even seem to know or understand just who exactly Morna Conall was.

He'd overreacted. He knew the lass wasn't lying, but the shock of her words had just been too much.

She'd met Morna and Jerry only a few nights ago. Yet he'd seen their lifeless bodies months ago. How was this possible?

It wasn't.

So, which of their realities was true?

Paton walked over to the front castle steps and sat down as he placed his head in his hands. All he'd seen on the isle the day the fae released him was forever burned into his mind. But for the first time, some part of him began to doubt all of it.

Was it possible the fae had fooled him? Could their last act of torture against him have been to make him believe he'd lost everyone when he hadn't? If so, what did that mean for Kate and the others who would be awaiting his return? Had the fae done the same to them and made them believe he was dead? Did they believe he'd abandoned them and their life there on his own accord?

No. He couldn't allow himself to believe it. He couldn't allow himself to hope that everyone was still alive. If the belief of their survival took root within him and he found it to be untrue, he wasn't sure he could recover from the pain of it a second time.

But how could Morna and Jerry's presence be explained?

He thought silently, as the rain began to fall. He didn't move. Instead, he allowed the drops to soak through his clothes as he turned over the possibilities until his mind hurt from the effort.

No explanation made sense to him—except the one he was wholly unwilling to allow himself to believe.

None of this would do him any good. There was already so much that required his attention—the arrival of guests he needed to woo into an alliance of marriage, Miren's husband, the ardent longing he felt each time he thought of or looked at the strange time-traveling lass who now stood inside his bedroom. Not to mention, the men scattered throughout his village intent on killing her.

Laird Morton's stakeout of his village couldn't continue. While he knew the importance of maintaining peace with Laird Morton, he couldn't very well allow the laird's men to dominate his territory in such a way for long. He would make a trip into the village today, and new terms to their agreement would be set.

His first betrothal candidate would arrive in a few days. Laird Morton and his men would have to be gone before then.

Oh, how his head ached from the weight of all of it. How much simpler his life had been when he was just a lad on the isle with Nicol and the other men.

Everything would have to be dealt with in its time, but for now, he longed for distraction, and only one thing would satisfy the need churning inside him.

Dripping wet from the rain, Paton kicked off his boots as soon as he re-entered the castle, ignoring Clara's screams at him to disrobe in the entryway so he didn't leave a trail across the stone floors of the castle.

He'd scarcely heard the old woman's pleas, as only one thing occupied his mind.

The lass wouldn't deny him. There'd been tension between the two of them the night before, he was sure of it. He knew the way a woman looked when she wanted a man, and he could see it in Olivia's gaze every time they locked eyes.

He threw open the door to his room and stepped inside, his breath ragged and his cock hard as Olivia turned toward him with a gasp.

I didn't leave the bedroom when Paton did. Some part of me knew he would return once he'd cooled off from whatever had rattled him so. But when he did return, and the door crashed open behind me with such force that I jumped as I whirled around toward him, it only took one glance at him to know that nothing about him was calmer.

Instead, water dripped from his soaked kilt onto the floor,

pooling at his feet. His linen shirt, now see-through from water, clung to his muscles in a way that allowed me to see the rapid rise and fall of his chest as he stared at me, his eyes dark and needy.

"Are you…" I could hardly bring myself to speak to him. Just looking at him now, seeing how different he looked from any time before, filled me with nerves and a longing that seemed unbearable. "Are you okay?"

He shook his head and more water flicked off him as he stepped fully inside the room, closed the door, and bolted the lock.

"Nae, lass. I am no'."

Was he about to charge me? If he did, how would I respond?

It only took me about one second to answer my own question. I would tear my own clothes off and spread myself wide to take him. There was no way I was going to let myself pass on an opportunity like this if he wanted it.

But still unsure as to what exactly was running through Paton's mind, I tried to steady my voice as I spoke to him again.

"What happened?"

He ignored me as he walked close to the fire and threw on another log before removing his shirt and ringing it out onto the floor near the flames.

"I am no' accustomed to laying me intentions out so plainly for a lass, but I doona think I can do this without telling ye the truth."

I swallowed. "Okay…"

He faced me, his jaw tight, his nipples hard, as he continued to breathe hard and fast.

"In the many months before I returned home, I slept with a good many lassies, Olivia. I would take them in me arms, and love them until sunup, and once they were sated and sleeping, I would leave for the next village without another word."

I swallowed again as he took one step toward me.

"When I was with the fae, they would come to me and beg for me to please them, and they would please me in return, but they are an unfeeling lot, so 'twas easy to cast emotion aside for the sake of shared pleasure."

I stared back at him blankly. I'd heard nothing of any fae. I wasn't even sure what that was, but at that moment, I didn't care one bit.

He continued, and took one more step, shortening the space between us.

"Ye intend to leave here when we find a way for ye to go home, aye?"

I nodded.

"And ye do know that I must marry another soon, aye?"

I nodded again.

"Ye are no' like the others, lass. I've spoken to ye at length, I've laughed with ye. I care for yer safety, and I feel a connection to ye just as I have felt with every lass I've e'er known from yer strange, distant time. No' only that, but I doona have the option of leaving for another village once we have had our way with one another. Ye shall have to stay here, with me, for months to come."

I continued to nod like a bobble head.

"Lass, I want to run me lips over every inch of yer skin. I lied to ye last night. I did peek at yer arse, and 'tis the bonniest arse I've e'er seen. I want to gather it in me hands as I lift ye to the bed and bury meself inside ye. But I feel we must make an agreement before we proceed."

Apparently, my brain had broken completely, and the only thing I could do was nod.

"No matter how much we enjoy each other's company, no matter how good this act between us shall inevitably be, our lives are spinning us in separate directions. We canna fall in love with one another. Do ye agree?"

I swallowed, and my voice cracked as I spoke for the first time since he'd begun his speech to me.

"Yes. We won't fall in love. We can't. I have a life back home, and your family needs you here."

He smiled and reached for the pin on his kilt.

"Do ye want me, lass?"

"Yes."

With one quick flick, his kilt fell to the floor, and he stood before me naked, his erection throbbing and ready as my center grew slick at the sight of him. The room began to spin as I forgot to breathe.

"Good. Ye canna know how badly I've burned for ye since the moment I laid eyes on ye."

I barely had time to inhale before his lips were on me and we crashed together in a frenzy unlike anything I'd experienced in my life.

CHAPTER 28

God, the lass felt good in his arms. The way she kissed him, the way her hair smelled as he nibbled at her neck, the way her breast felt in his hand as he cupped the outside of her dress. Every bit of it just increased his desire for her. He ached to be inside her, to feel her arch beneath him as they moved together.

"Turn around, lass." Paton whispered in her ear before grazing her earlobe with his teeth. "I must get ye out of this dress or I shall die from need of ye."

Breathlessly, she tore her lips away from his cheek and spun her back toward him, as he deftly undid the buttons that kept him from seeing her. Once they were undone, he gripped Olivia's shoulders and spun her back toward him as the gown pooled at her feet.

A needy groan escaped from his throat as his eyes raked over her naked body.

"Ye are stunning, lass. Every bit of ye."

She smiled at him, a lock of her hair falling down over her face in a way that caused his cock to pump upward in yearning as he pulled her near him. She jumped into his arms, and just as he'd promised her, he took her rear into his hands as he carried her to the bed and lay her back upon the blankets.

He shifted so that he lay beside her. And as he bent to kiss her once more, he allowed his hand to travel downward until he found her center. His fingers moved quickly as she shook beneath him, moaning in between kisses as her breath came hot against his mouth. Just as she neared her release, he stopped and slipped his finger all the way inside. She was wet and ready for him. Just as he was about to roll over on top of her, she surprised him by pushing herself up and moving to straddle him on the bed.

"Are you ready?"

No other lassie he'd been with had ever taken such initiative. He glanced down at his erection and smiled at her.

"Aye, lass. I doona think I can bear it a moment longer."

She arched her back as she slid herself over him, enveloping his shaft in a way so pleasurable he nearly burst from the sensation of it. It took everything inside him to hold back. He wanted this to last. He wanted to savor every minute.

Unable to keep from kissing her, Paton rose from his horizontal position, claiming her mouth with his own as he wrapped his arms around her. They moved together in an embrace that sent them both to dizzying heights. When she cried out in pleasure and began to shake against him from her own release, he rolled over and laid her down on the bed while taking his time to pull one of her nipples into his mouth before plunging into her once more.

He allowed himself to build to his own crescendo now.

When she rocked against him, he felt himself begin to pulse inside her, as ecstasy rolled through him. Once finished, he pulled her into his arms. When she looked up at him with a smile, he knew he'd just made the biggest mistake of his life.

How could he avoid falling in love with a lass like her?

Paton never napped during the day, but he'd been unable to pull himself away from the lass. Instead, he held her against his chest as she dozed throughout the morning, only stirring at a soft knock followed by Chambers' gruff voice at the door.

"Paton, I doona wish to disturb ye, but Miren was out in the garden when she noticed Laird Morton riding toward the castle. I thought ye might wish to be downstairs when he entered."

Good. Thayne's visit would save him a trip into the village.

"Thank ye, Chambers. I shall be down shortly."

Quickly, he gave Olivia a gentle shake to wake her.

"I must go, lass. Doona leave this room until someone comes to tell ye 'tis safe to do so. It seems Laird Morton has paid us another visit. Come and bolt the door behind me when I leave."

Once she'd given him her word that she would stay put, Paton dressed quickly and hurried downstairs. No sooner had his feet touched the castle entryway than Laird Morton entered the castle unannounced. He looked terrible—as hungover as Olivia should've been.

"Laird Morton."

"Laird Buchannan."

"'Tis it customary for ye to enter another's home without knocking?"

Thayne chuckled once as he brushed past Paton and made his way into the sitting room, uninvited.

"I saw that yer new chef had seen me. I knew that ye were told I was coming."

Paton doubled his stride so that he could step in front of Thayne and halt his path. He spoke through a tight jaw as he glowered at the old man.

"Still, doona do so again. I doubt verra much that ye would respond kindly to such behavior from me or any other. If ye enter me home again without being escorted in by me or one of my staff, I shall—"

Laird Morton cut him off, "What, lad? Ye shall cut off my hand as yer brother did to that poor man in the village? Those who found him say 'tis lucky he's alive."

"Bram had reason to do as he did. Murray regularly beat his wife, and Bram was a witness to it."

Thayne continued, as the tension between them built. "And just how did he happen to witness such an act? 'Twas it because he was invited inside the man's home, or did he enter much as I have done?"

"He only entered because he heard the lass scream. Ye heard no such trouble before ye stepped within these walls."

"It seems a convenient thing, that the lass ye need here to cook yer meals is the verra same lass whose husband ye and Bram dinna see fit."

Thayne was trying to bait him, to cause him to lash out in anger. With the possibility of combining their families now gone, Paton knew Laird Morton would seek another way to complicate the debt his family owed.

"Tis business that is on me territory, Laird Morton. No' yers. None of this is any of yer concern. Is that why ye've come? To speak on Murray Black's behalf? Do ye even know the man?"

Thayne laughed and moved to sit down on the other side of the room. "No, I doona know the man, nor do I care to. In truth, 'tis no' me concern what ye or yer brother do with men like him. 'Tis only that robbing a man of his hand is a violent act, an act committed to protect another from a life they dinna want. I canna help but wonder if a family prone to such violence might also have it within them to kill another if they thought it might be in service of their sister."

Paton kept his tone calm and his face still as he moved to sit across from Laird Morton.

"We've already discussed this, Thayne. I wouldna have sent a lass to kill yer son."

"Precisely, lad. Mayhap I have accused the wrong person. Mayhap the lass convinced Lanrick that she wasna mad and he let her go. Me boy was kind that way. Foolish. But kind. Mayhap the girl had nothing to do with Lanrick's death. Mayhap he was attacked once he was alone in the forest."

While it pleased him to know that perhaps Laird Morton was redirecting his vengeance away from Olivia, the path Thayne now wished to tread would only lead to destruction for both their territories. He would have to do everything in his power to stop it from escalating.

"I promise ye, Thayne, None inside this castle—no' me, nor Bram, nor any of me servants murdered yer son."

Laird Morton stared at him, seemingly trying to gauge his sincerity, after a long moment, the old man spoke. "All I can do is take yer word for it. But let me assure ye this, if I find out that ye or anyone of yer household was involved with this, the two territories of this isle will be at war."

"Then we shall both rest easily tonight, for I give ye me word that ye will find no such thing."

Laird Morton stood, but Paton held out a hand to stop him.

"Wait, a moment, Thayne. There is more I wish to discuss with ye. I canna allow ye or yer men to stay on this side of the isle forever. I know ye need to hunt for the lass that killed Lanrick. I would want the same. But ye are making villagers uneasy with yer men stationed around watching everyone's every movement. Ye may search for three more days, and then I must insist that ye return to yer home. If we e'er see the lass, we shall apprehend her and deliver her to ye, but if no', this matter must come to an end."

"No. 'Tis not enough time."

Paton remained firm. "It must be. I have visitors arriving from the mainland four days from now. I'll no' have them involved in any of this."

"Visitors?"

"Aye. 'Tis long past time that I marry. I have invited Laird McKinsley's clan to stay in the hopes that there may be something between his daughter and me."

Thayne laughed as he shook his head. "Ah. Now, I see. This is how ye intend to pay the debt."

"Everyone knows 'tis time for me to take a wife. If me marriage ensures the success of both families involved, then I canna see the harm in that. There were no conditions as to where the funds come from, aye?"

Thayne's smile disappeared in a flash as he stood. "Nae, lad. Ye are clever, I give ye that. Good luck to ye. Ye must know that if ye are unable to succeed in this scheme that there is only one other solution to seeing this debt paid if ye doona come up with the funds in time."

Paton crossed his arms, no longer interested in Laird Morton's games. All he wanted was the man out of his home and off his land.

"Lanrick is no' here to marry yer sister, but if I am no' paid, then I shall lay claim on all of Buchannan territory, and if ye doona willingly surrender it, I shall gather me men and take it by force."

A cold knot of dread settled in Paton's stomach as Laird Morton walked away. His plan to find a wife had to succeed, and in truth, he had no confidence that it would.

"I am no' worried, Laird Morton. Every coin will be repaid. Now get out of me home and never enter here unescorted again. And if yer men are no' off my land within three days, I shall see that they are removed."

CHAPTER 29

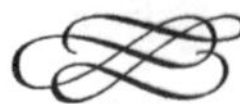

Three Days Ride from Cagair Castle, Scotland

Davy reached into his satchel and felt for the coins that remained. There was still more than enough for him to stop and seek proper lodging for the night. After three nights under the stars, he longed for a proper bed and a warm meal.

The smells coming from the inn and ale house caused his stomach to growl as he approached, but when he saw the crowd of people gathered inside, his hopes sank. Still, it would be better to ask and be turned away than to sleep outdoors when there might have been an empty bed. Bracing himself for rejection, he entered and walked over to the counter, where a plump woman with the reddest cheeks saw him approach.

"Can I help ye with something, lad? How about a warm stew and potato?"

"Aye, is there any chance of ye still having lodging available?"

She smiled and hope blossomed inside him once more. "Aye. Though ye doona have others with ye outside, do ye? We've only one room vacant. The other two have been filled for the past three nights by the same man and his family. Though I think they head back out on the road tomorrow."

"'Tis only me."

"Perfect, lad. Ye look as if ye need a rest. If ye'd like, I can have a meal brought to yer room. 'Tis the first one on the left at the top of the stairs."

"Lass, I could kiss ye."

Her horrified expression nearly made him burst out laughing, but he quickly hurried to reassure her instead.

"But I promise ye I willna do so."

"Good. Now, get yerself upstairs and kick yer feet up. Warm food will be along soon."

Smiling every step, Davy made his way to the small, but suitable, room. Kicking his boots off by the door, he didn't bother removing his coat as he collapsed backwards on the bed.

"Da, why canna I sleep with Jack and Isla. 'Tis unfair that I must stay with ye and mother."

The young child's voice traveled easily through the inn's thin walls, and Davy sat up straight at the names mentioned.

It couldn't be. Surely, the chances were too slim.

On the off chance he was right, he scooted back in the bed, and placed his ear against the wall.

"Because ye willna sleep. Ye will terrorize yer siblings until ye all get in a fight and one of ye ends up with a bruise that I doona wish to explain to anyone else. Ye shall stay here with yer mother and me. And that is all we shall speak of it."

The man's voice was unmistakable. It was Gawen—Buchannan Castle's missing chef.

Davy didn't even bother putting on his boots before stepping into the hallway and nearly knocking the woman over that was bringing him food.

"Och, excuse me, lass. Ye may set the food right inside."

She looked at him hesitantly as she leaned forward into his room and set it down on the table.

"Is there something I can help ye with?"

"Nae, lass. I'm fine."

He waited until she turned to head back downstairs before walking the few paces over to Gawen's room and lifting his hand to knock.

The door swung open almost immediately as Davy looked down to see Gawen's youngest child staring up at him.

"I know ye. Ye work with Da."

Gawen suddenly appeared behind the child. Davy was certain he could see the blood visibly drain from the man's face.

"Davy, what...what are ye doing here? Did, did Paton send ye after me?"

Davy reached through the doorway to pat his friend on the shoulder.

"Nae, lad. 'Tis fate, it seems. I am on another errand and heard yer voice through the wall. My room is just the next one over. I would like to speak to ye, though. We've all been so worried."

Gawen brushed past him into the hall before motioning for Davy to follow him.

"Not here, Davy. Can we go into yer room?"

He nodded and followed Gawen inside. As he shut the door behind them, he looked over to see Gawen crying.

"Gawen, what is amiss with ye? What's happened?"

"I am glad that ye've found me. I have been living in misery, lad. I canna live with meself for what I've done."

Davy frowned and pulled out one of the two chairs situated around the small table where his food grew cold.

"Sit down, man. Take a breath. Whate'er has happened, it canna be as bad as ye think."

The man shook his head in disagreement. "But 'tis. Why else would I leave? Why else would I uproot my family and lead them away to I doona know where?"

"Alright, lad. Just tell me. Mayhap I can help ye."

"Ye must know that I dinna want to do it. I dinna have a choice."

"Whatever 'tis, I believe ye. Now do ye intend to tell me?"

Gawen nodded and closed his eyes as he began to speak. "Several weeks ago, I was in the village gathering supplies for the week, when I was approached by Laird Morton. I dinna know why he was on Buchannan land, but he dinna give me a chance to ask as he pulled me away from me horse. He and his men dragged me into the trees and threatened me life and the lives of me children if I dinna do what he asked of me."

Davy's eyes grew wide with horror. "What did he ask of ye?"

"He asked me to steal the late Laird Buchannan's signet ring. And I did."

Everything made sense now in an instant. "Och, Gawen, ye canna be angry with yerself. Laird Morton doesna make idle threats. Ye dinna have a choice."

"Aye, but I have caused pain to a family that has shown me naught but kindness. I promise ye, though, I only intend to see me family settled somewhere safe, then I will write to Paton and tell him the truth of all of it."

"There is no need. I shall ride back at once and tell him meself. He willna be angry with ye."

"Ye do know what this means though, doona ye, Davy?"

"The late laird ne'er agreed to marry Ella to Lanrick if he couldna repay his debt."

Gawen opened his eyes and locked them with his own as he shook his head.

"No' only that. The late laird ne'er owed Laird Morton a single coin. There was ne'er any debt. All of Laird Morton's scheme is a lie."

CHAPTER 30

Buchannan Castle, Scotland

Once Laird Morton left, I didn't see much of Paton for most of the day. Instead, I was finally able to properly meet his sister, Ella, and she occupied most of my time by showing me every inch of the castle. The young girl was immensely likeable, and I learned much about Paton through my conversations with her.

When Paton had been so convinced that magic was inside me, his ardent questioning had given me no time to properly ask him what he meant when he said that he had once possessed such powers. Ella helped fill in some of the gaps. She explained that Paton had been gone for most of her life, having only recently returned home, but I could sense that there were things she didn't wish to tell me about Paton's time away.

Perhaps, she herself didn't know, but I truly got the feeling that it was more that she didn't believe it was her story to tell.

I could understand that. But I hoped I would have a chance to ask Paton my ever-growing list of questions about him sometime soon.

She also informed me of all that had happened in the village with Bram, Miren, and her husband. Signs that something was amiss with her were evident from the first, and I found myself so grateful that she was now free from the horrid situation and, much like me, safe inside Buchannan Castle.

When I did see Paton again it was toward the end of dinner. He sat down to eat as everyone else at the table was finishing up. I stayed with him as the others bid us both goodnight, not only because I'd missed him during the day, but also because I wasn't quite sure where my place was in the castle now that I was no longer injured.

"You look as if you're carrying the weight of the world."

He gave me a half-hearted smile as he lifted a bowl of lukewarm stew up to his lips. He took a hearty taste before answering me.

"I am worried, lass. If I doona secure a marriage before the agreed upon deadline, I shall be the man who turned this beautiful land over to a man who doesna deserve the half he currently has."

I couldn't imagine how much pressure he felt. To be forced to resolve a situation not of his own making. It wasn't fair.

"Do you have reason to think you will be unable to secure a marriage?"

"Aye. Many. While Skye is beautiful land, 'tis not the most strategic territory to combine with another family. We are not close at hand to lend help if needed. Not only that, but if the family loves their daughter, they are sending her away to a land that ensures they will rarely see her. I am also new here. While me father was a man of many talents, fostering relationships outside of his own kin wasna one of them. Many families throughout Scotland have deep roots, families they know and trust with whom they will want to secure ties. No' me. Why would they trust me with their daughters? Why would they give me the money I need to stop Laird Morton?"

"They will sense your sincerity, Paton. And every one of their daughters will wish to wed you, I'm certain."

He smiled at me, and leaned back in his chair. "Ye are kind, lass. Though I am no' so sure 'tis true."

He truly had no idea how good looking he actually was.

"I'm sure." I yawned as a wave of sleepiness came over me. "Paton, did Clara have a chance to clean my old room? I'm healed now, so I should probably let you have your room back."

He pushed his bowl away and leaned forward until his elbows were on the table. "Aye, 'tis clean, but I've spent a great deal of time thinking this over today, lass, and I have come to a decision. Ye are to make me room yer own for the duration of yer time here."

While I yearned to spend more time with him, I knew such an arrangement would be a terrible idea. We both liked one another. The sex was amazing. Spending every night in the same room together, in the same bed, would make keeping our agreement impossible.

"I'm not sure that's a great idea."

"Nor I, lass, but 'tis what we must do. Now that Miren has moved into the castle permanently, we have not a single extra room when we account for those that are coming with Laird MacKaslin's clan. And ye are to stay hidden, for all of our guests will inevitably have seen yer likeness in the posters Laird Morton has placed of ye all over the village."

The thought of my face on a wanted poster caused me to visibly shiver, and Paton immediately rushed to reassure me.

"Ye are safe here, lass. I promise ye that, but we must keep ye hidden once our guests arrive. The best place to do so will be me bedchamber, as none would enter there without me as their escort. But ye are right, lass. After this morning, I doona trust myself to sleep next to ye night after night and no' fall for ye. I shall sleep elsewhere."

I frowned at him. "You just said there were no available rooms."

"I dinna say I would be sleeping in a room. I said I would be sleeping elsewhere."

"Are you sure?"

He gave me a firm nod as he pushed himself away from the table. "Verra, lass. Ye are a danger. I sensed it the moment I saw ye."

He gave me a smile, his dimples making my stomach all fluttery as he left me in the dining hall alone.

Sleep deprivation would kill him if he had to remain in this chair for the next weeks, but that seemed preferable to the trouble he would be in if he allowed himself to fall in love with Olivia.

He knew there were empty rooms in the castle now, but after the work Clara had put into readying them for guests, he knew better than to mess one up by sleeping in one of them tonight.

Instead, he shifted back and forth in the chair, that no matter how he positioned himself was much too small for him. His neck ached dreadfully, and his arms kept falling asleep as he tried to get comfortable.

For hours his miserable dance continued. When a whisper reached his ear from the darkness behind him, his need for sleep suddenly outweighed his resolve to keep as much distance between him and Olivia.

"I can't sleep, Paton. Would you come upstairs and rub my feet again until I fall asleep?"

He couldn't help but smile. They both knew very well that if he joined her upstairs, he would be rubbing much more than her feet.

To hell with it. These were his last days of freedom. If things went according to plan, he would soon be married to a woman he barely knew. A marriage of love was too much to ask for in his current situation. If love could find him now—even if it was brief—he suddenly saw that he had to take it.

Too much grief had filled his life. He would be a fool to deny himself joy.

And the lass, Olivia, was the very definition of joy for him.

"Aye, lass. But ye must forgive me if my hands stray upwards."

She laughed in the darkness and in an instant, his cock grew hard.

"I'm counting on it, Paton. Now please come to bed."

CHAPTER 31

Their time was up, and still he, nor any of his men, had caught sight of the lass he sought. Where could the bitch have gone? Could she have fled here? Could she be hiding in his own territory at this very moment?

It was possible. She would have to be a fool to have remained in the very woods—in the very village—where so many were looking for her. And no fool would've been able to get the best of his dear, Lanrick.

It was with this in mind, that Laird Morton chose to acquiesce to Paton's demands. They'd searched all they could on Buchannan land. It was time to expand their search to their own territory.

Gathering his men, they began the ride back to the main road that was shared between the two sides of the isle, and as his men filed in along the road back to Morton Castle, he could hear a rider in the distance thundering toward them.

Whoever it was seemed to be in a very big hurry. He couldn't help but wonder why.

Halting his men, Laird Morton rode to the front, squinting as the rider came into view.

He couldn't remember the lad's name, but he knew precisely where he'd seen the man before. He was Paton's right-hand man, and clearly, he'd been on an errand for the laird.

"Halt, sir!" He called out to the rider as he neared him, and slowly the man reined in his steed.

The rider gave Laird Morton a courteous nod as he reached him.

"Laird Morton. Are ye returning home, then?"

"Aye, and where have ye been?"

He didn't miss the way the man hesitated, and he knew whatever the man would say next would be a lie. Had he been sent to smuggle the murderer off the isle? Could this man be the reason they'd yet to find her?

"I doona think it any of yer concern, sir. I am no' on yer land. Now, if ye will excuse me."

With a flick of his wrist, Thayne motioned for his men to stop him.

"Ye are wrong, lad. This road is shared, which means Paton and I both make the rules along this road. Ye seem to be in a hurry, but I am afraid ye shall be detained."

Turning his back to the man, he spoke to his head guard.

"See the lad back to the castle, and chain him downstairs. Doona hurt him. We will only do that if he doesna tell me what 'tis I wish to know."

"What is a fae, Paton?"

My face pressed flush against his chest as he held me, I felt him look down at me, and when he answered his tone sounded surprised.

"Have I spoke of the fae in front of ye?"

"Yes. Before we had sex for the first time. You told me that you'd spent time with them and they'd taken pleasure from you."

"I must confess, lass. I was in such pain from wanting ye, I can barely remember anything I said to ye."

It took a little prodding, but over the course of the evening, Paton answered all the burning questions my time with Ella had left me with.

All that he'd been through—all that he'd lost—endeared him to me even more. His tone gave away how much he still grieved, but he'd not allowed himself to become bitter or jaded by it. He was still kind and generous. He could still laugh and make jokes.

I had no confidence that I would've come out of that situation in the same condition.

When all was said and we both began to drift to sleep, I whispered up to him before lifting myself to give him a good night kiss.

"I don't know why you were worried I would fall for you. I don't even like you a little bit."

He laughed against my hair and gave my rear a gentle squeeze as I turned away from him to let him spoon me.

"Aye, I canna stand the sight of ye."

Warm, safe, and blissfully happy, we drifted to sleep wrapped in each other's arms.

CHAPTER 32

The morning Paton's first wife candidate was supposed to show up, I sulked around the castle unable to enjoy my last few moments of freedom. Any minute, Chambers would see the clan coming up the castle path and would holler a warning at me to make myself scarce. I should've been making the most of my time. Instead, I roamed around the castle irritable, snappy, and full of dread. And to make matters worse, I knew I had absolutely no right to be any of those things.

I was still intent on returning home. I had to. There was no other option for me. Of course Paton had to continue with the plans he'd set in place before I showed up here and complicated everything. I had no claim on him. And yet, I already hated whoever it was that would become his betrothed.

In only a few nights, Paton felt like mine. More than Peter ever had or could. There in Paton's bed, in his arms, not only during our lovemaking, but in the hours that followed where we laughed and talked, I knew why I'd been so dissatisfied in my previous relationship. I had been right to suspect that there could be so much more.

But Paton wasn't meant for me. If he had been, I would've been born in his time, or he in mine. All of this was a mistake, and sooner or later, it would all have to end.

As I roamed around the castle, I eventually made my way to the kitchen but stopped just outside as I heard low, whispered voices inside.

"Bram, please doona look at me that way. I canna allow ye to kiss me again."

"Tell me why no', Miren. Havna we both been through enough? Do we no' deserve happiness if 'tis right in front of us?"

I was too close to the situation now to move. If I backed away, I feared they would hear me. If I stepped inside, I would interrupt something I had no desire to see end.

"I am married, Bram. Though I hope to ne'er see Murray Black again, in the eyes o' God, I am married. I think too much of ye to have ye sully yerself by throwing yer lot in with me."

"I doona give a damn what anyone thinks, Miren. Ye are the first lass to make me feel as if I can breathe again since Winifred. Tell me ye doona feel the same way."

I held my breath as I listened for her to answer him.

"I doona." Miren took a shaky breath before continuing. "For I have never felt the way I do for ye, Bram. While ye say I give ye breath. I seem to be unable to breathe in yer presence."

Something akin to a sob escaped from Bram before the sound of their breathy kissing reached me in the hallway, and I knew my only option was to try to leave now. Eavesdropping on their conversation was bad enough. Listening to them make out was just straight creepy.

My sour mood lifted somewhat as I tip-toed away from the kitchen. I was happy for Miren. For Bram, as well. They deserved some love in their lives—even if it was a little inconvenient for them both.

As Chambers spotted me in the hallway and said the words that signaled the start of my imprisonment here, I couldn't help but wonder why it was so easy for me to believe that others deserved happiness, but I was still so sure the happiness I'd found here had to be some sort of cosmic mistake.

Maybe I'd been thinking about it all wrong? Maybe it was wrong of me to believe that if Paton was meant for me, we would've been born in the same time. Maybe, the opposite was true. Maybe I traveled through time because we were.

Lady Caitlin was beautiful, to be sure, but the way the lass stared at him—her eyes never glancing elsewhere—made him uneasy. Her eyes raked over him, up and down, back and forth while she ate. He could all but see her undressing him with her eyes.

Before the meal was even over, he'd already made the decision that this lass would be unbearable to live with. He wouldna be asking Laird MacKaslin for his daughter's hand.

"I was pleased to receive yer invitation, and I canna wait to speak to ye more, but the journey has tired us all. I hope ye willna think it rude if we retire now."

Paton couldn't have been happier with the laird's suggestion.

"O'course. There is much time for us to visit. I will have Chambers escort ye all to yer bedchambers. We've already placed yer trunks inside. Fresh baths and fires should be ready."

For the first time all evening, Lady Caitlin spoke, and the sound of her voice was as grating as the way she stared.

"I wish for ye to escort me, Laird Buchannan."

Paton froze at the request, unsure of how to respond. It was untoward and improper for her to suggest such a thing in front of anyone. But he couldn't believe that she'd made such a request in front of her father.

"Caitlin!" Laird MacKaslin was quick to chastise his daughter. "Ye know 'tis scandalous to suggest such a thing. But…" he paused, and a knot formed in Paton's stomach. "I shall allow it." The old man paused and leaned in close to him. "We have had trouble finding a suitable match for Caitlin, Laird Buchannan. 'Tis my hope that ye shall take the time to truly get to know her. She has a good heart when ye take the time to see it."

Gobsmacked, Paton glanced over at his brother for help, but Bram simply looked like he was on the edge of laughter. Had the lass' father truly just hinted that he wanted him to bed his daughter?

Just as Miren moved to gather up dishes around the table, he reached out and placed a hand on her arm to stop her.

"Verra well. I shall show the lass to her room, but I shall bring Lady Miren as escort. I'll not have any unfair rumors spread about yer daughter while she is under my roof."

His answer seemed to please the man, as he smiled, rose from the table, and gathered his wife before following Chambers out of the room.

Caitlin stood quickly, and as she neared him, he leaned over to plead in Miren's ear.

"Doona ye dare leave me alone with the lass for a moment, do ye understand?"

Miren nodded and patted his hand in reassurance as he finally released her arm.

Knowing he had no choice, he extended his arm so that Cailtin would take it.

"Are ye ready, lass? Ye must be tired after the journey here. I know 'tis not an easy trip to make."

"I am not tired in the least."

He forced himself to yawn in an attempt to dissuade the lass of any ideas she had about where this walk down the hallway might lead.

"Miren, why doona ye lead the way?"

Blessedly, Miren walked quickly, and he matched her pace as he hurried Caitlin along to her room. Once they reached the room in question, he had to pry her fingers from his arm.

"Here ye are, lass. I shall bid ye goodnight."

Caitlin's tone lifted into a whine that made the hairs on his arms stand on end.

"Doona ye wish to show me around the room?"

"'Tis a small room, lass. There is nothing to show ye. Now, if ye will excuse me."

He all but ran from the room in his haste to get back to his own bedchamber.

Back to Olivia.

If this first visit was any sort of indication of how the rest would be, Laird Morton was all but guaranteed to become owner of some of the finest land in all of Scotland.

CHAPTER 33

"So, a no-go, then?"

It was wrong of me to feel so delighted by the miserable look on Paton's face as he entered his bedchamber much earlier than expected, but I couldn't help it. Had he looked happy, it would've broken my heart more than I wished to admit to him.

"If I have e'er made a lass feel the way that young girl made me feel, I shall forever be ashamed for it."

I sat up in the bed as I pulled back a corner of the blankets for him as he disrobed and crawled inside, kissing me on the cheek as he did so.

"How do you mean?"

"She stared at me for the entirety of the evening as if I were the steak she wished to eat for dinner."

I snorted as I tried to suppress a laugh. "I'm sure that's exactly what she wanted to do." I turned to kiss him. "I mean, I can't blame her."

"I wish ye could hear her voice, lass. 'Tis the most dreadful sound I've ever heard. Had we dogs, they would've howled at the moon in response to it."

"I feel as if you're probably being a little too harsh on the poor girl."

"No, lass. Her Da all but asked me to bed her. I dinna even need to mention a betrothal. He suggested it right at the end of supper."

Panic settled in my gut. "You didn't say yes, right?"

"I said nothing. I canna do it. Not to this lass."

"There will be others."

He reached for me, turning me over as he pulled me on top of him, his lips pressed close to my ear.

"Mayhap so, lass, but for tonight, there is only ye."

I lifted my nightgown, and in a way that was already so familiar to us both, guided him inside me as I began to move on top of him. He reached for the bottom of my nightgown and deftly pulled it over my head as he leaned forward to pull one of my nipples deep into his mouth. I groaned and threw my head back as I lost myself in the sensation I couldn't seem to get enough of.

Neither of us heard the bedchamber door open. While I couldn't say how long she stood there, it was only after I orgasmed that Paton tore his gaze away from me long enough to notice Caitlin standing all the way inside his room.

He screamed, startling me as he bucked me off him, and rolled me over beside him before throwing the blankets on my head.

"Cailtlin, lass, what the hell are ye doing in me bedchamber? How did ye even know where 'tis?"

"I watched where ye headed once ye left me so rudely in my

room. I thought ye would wish for me to seek ye out, but I see ye already have a whore in yer bed."

"Leave this room this instant, lass, and I willna say a word of this to yer father."

I lay there shaking beneath the blankets as I waited for her to leave. Thankfully, my back had been toward her, and with the low lighting in the room, I didn't think there was any way that she could've made out my face.

"Doona worry about that, Laird Buchannan. I shall tell him myself."

She slammed the door behind her on the way out, and in an effort to ease the tension, I said the first thing that came to mind.

"You got your wish. I got to hear her voice, and you weren't wrong. My ears shall ache for weeks."

Laughing, Paton slipped beneath the covers with me as we lay there cocooned in the delicious warmth of the blankets.

"I told ye. Now come to me, lass so we can finish what we started. There is naught I can do about this mess until the morrow."

"I doona begrudge a man his pleasures, Laird Buchannan. A man may do what he wishes in his own home, but I do take issue with ye inviting a whore into the castle while me wife and daughter are here."

Paton's eyes grew wide as he stared back at Laird McKaslin over breakfast. He'd never met a man who spoke so bluntly. At least his daughter came by her strange behaviors honestly.

"Perhaps we should speak of this alone." Paton glanced over

at Bram and Ella as he felt his face flush red with embarrassment.

"Nonsense. If ye are brash enough to escort a whore in while ye have guests, ye should be bold enough no' to hide it."

"I dinna have a whore inside the castle, sir. I have ne'er had the need to pay any lass to get her into my bed."

The old laird gruffed at him, disbelievingly. "Then who did my daughter see in yer bed? 'Twas not one of me servants."

All that crossed his mind before he spoke was his desire to protect Olivia. "Nae. 'Twas one of mine."

Miren dropped the dish she carried from the kitchen at his statement, and he knew full well that she would know that all would assume the lass he spoke of was her. He would pay for the lie later, but for now, it was his only choice.

Laird McKaslin directed his attention toward Miren. "I suppose ye are the one then?"

Paton rose from the table to save her from speaking. "Ye will not address her in this. As ye have said, 'tis me house and I shall do in it as I please."

"Verra well, and we shall be leaving today. I think we've all seen enough of what the Buchannan clan is about to know we want no part in any of it."

"O'course. I shall have yer trunks readied at once. Safe travels on yer journey home."

Good riddance to all of them. Paton hoped he never had to see any of them ever again. He rose from the table as he gave the laird a curt nod.

CHAPTER 34

Paton heard the angry footsteps behind him, but as he turned to face whoever it was approaching him, a fist slammed into the side of his face, knocking him off balance before he could make out who his assailant was.

"Could ye no' just let me have her? I know that ye doona love her, Paton. Mayhap ye did as a boy, but ye doona now. Could ye no' just leave the lass alone?"

Straightening himself, Paton reached up to rub his cheek as he swallowed the urge to knock his brother straight back on his arse.

"What are ye talking aboot, Bram? I havena seen ye spend more than the briefest of moments with Olivia."

"Olivia?" Bram's expression contorted in confusion.

"Who else would ye be speaking of?"

"Miren, o'course! Ye said plainly enough in front of everyone at breakfast that ye slept with her."

"Bram," He reached out to grab his brother's arm. "I only

implied 'twas Miren to protect Olivia. None can know she is here, remember? I havna touched Miren. Ye are right in all that ye said. I loved her once, but I doona now, and she doesna love me either."

Bram drew a ragged breath as his expression softened. "I…I am sorry. I doona know what came over me."

"Did ye no' think of asking Miren if 'twas true before ye chose to hit me?"

"I should have. As I said, I doona know why I behaved so brashly."

"I do. Ye love her."

He could see it in Bram because no matter how much he tried to deny it, he was also a man in love.

With the early departure of Paton's guests, I was once again given free rein of the castle. The respite from the confines of Paton's room would be brief. Almost as soon as the first clan's belongings were cleared out of the castle, a messenger arrived with notice that the next clan would be arriving in a few days.

I longed for fresh air and sunshine, but even though Lord Morton's men had supposedly returned to their own territory, I knew it was too risky. Eager to do something to keep myself busy, I wandered into the kitchen where Miren sat perched on a small wooden stool, her arms covered in flour as she kneaded dough.

"Would you like some help?"

"Do ye know how to cook, lass?"

Her expression told me that she fully expected me to say no.

"Cook? Not so much. Bake? Well, that's kind of my thing."

"Is it?" She smiled as I walked over to wash my hands in a small basin of water.

"Yes. That's what I used to do for a living back home, in my own time."

"Ye made bread?"

"I can make bread, though we never did very much of that. Lots of wedding cakes. Pies around holidays. Cookies. Sweets, mainly."

My time here had been the longest stretch of my life that I'd gone without baking something. And to my surprise, I was eager to get back to it.

"Do you have any sugar in the kitchen? And eggs?"

Miren bobbed her head over to what appeared to be a small shelf which served as a pantry.

"Aye, lass. 'Tis right over there."

"Would you mind if I try to put something sweet together for us to all have after dinner?"

"O'course no'. Let me know if ye need me to do anything. I am nearly finished with this."

As Miren continued to work, I walked over to the pantry and examined the ingredients. The sugar looked unlike what I was accustomed to, but it would be fine if the cake turned out a little less sweet than normal. I could make it work.

Gathering what I would need in my arms, I moved over to the side of the counter opposite from Miren and looked around for a bowl to mix my ingredients in. The task would be a true test of my abilities. With no gas oven and no nonstick pans, I would have to adjust about every bit of what I could usually do blindfolded. Still, I was up for the challenge. I was up for anything, really, that might take my mind off the man who seemed to occupy more and more of it all the time.

But rather than provide me a respite from my never-ending thoughts about Paton, Miren wasted no time diving in with questions I'd been doing my utmost to avoid.

"Ye've done well here, lass."

"Do you think so?"

She nodded, as she covered the dough she'd just worked with a cloth and walked over to dip her floured hands in water to clean them.

"Aye. While I canna pretend to know anything about yer own time, I know it must be quite different from ours. But still, it seems to me ye are flourishing here."

Was I?

Sure, I enjoyed everyone at the castle. My life before had been so small—comprised of only the bakery, Rory, and Peter. Here I truly felt as though I had friends. They'd all put themselves in danger to help me, right away, without question, and I couldn't help but feel like we'd all bonded as a result.

"I can't deny that I've enjoyed my time here. That first day, once the truth of what was happening really set in, I was certain I would be in a full-fledged panic every second until I got home. But now…a few more months here no longer seems very long at all."

"Have ye ever thought of staying? I doona think I am the only one within the castle that would be pleased if ye did."

Staying wasn't an option. Rory needed me. I couldn't abandon my sister.

"I can't."

"May I ask ye why?"

"My sister needs me."

"And why does she need ye? Ye've mentioned yer sister many times, Liv. And while I doona doubt yer love for her, are the two of ye no' meant to live yer own lives? Has it occurred to ye that mayhap ye were sent here because 'twas precisely where ye are meant to be?"

Had Miren somehow been listening in on the very same questions my subconscious mind had been tormenting me with for days?

"Why would I be meant to stay here, Miren?"

She crossed her arms in frustration as she returned to her stool to watch me work.

"Olivia, doona ye think I can see the way ye look at Paton when the two of ye are in a room together? Or the way he looks at ye? Ye are a fine match. I doona believe I have e'er seen Paton so happy. And believe me, there are few in this world who know Paton Buchannan better than I. For much of me life, I believed I would be lady of this castle."

Ah, so I'd been right the night I'd sensed a history between them. But from what I'd overheard between her and Bram, I knew it was safe to assume that all of that was long over and done with.

"Miren, if that were true…if I was sent back here to be with Paton, don't you think the timing is a little bit off? He has to marry another. It's the only way he can keep this land, this castle, from falling into the hands of Laird Morton. I can't stand in the way of that. Besides that, I will never be safe here as long as Laird Morton is alive. I can't very well be locked up in this castle forever."

She sighed.

"'Tis true that Laird Morton poses a challenge for ye both. But Paton doesna wish to wed another, Olivia. Take it from someone who knows just how much of yer life can be wasted by marrying someone ye doona love, he will regret it forever if he sacrifices his own heart for the sake of this land and castle. It may seem worth it to him now, but in the end, 'tis far too high a price."

"But what am I supposed to do about it, Miren? I can't be the one responsible for his family losing this place. I couldn't live with myself if he chose me over them. Besides, he's given me no reason to believe that he would choose me anyway. He's made no confession of love, he hasn't asked me to stay, he's made no mention of having Davy call off his search for another portal."

"Olivia, lass, in the span of only a few years, Paton has lost more than most ever shall. Can ye no' see that if he were to make himself that vulnerable to ye and ye dinna stay, 'twould destroy him? Once he admits his feelings, he again opens the door to the possibility of losing another he loves. He is a strong man, but even the strongest of men can only take so much."

"Okay, just for the sake of argument, let's say Paton and I choose to be together. What do we do about Laird Morton? About both the debt and the fact that I killed his son?"

She pushed herself off her perch and dusted her hands on her apron, as she moved to leave.

"I doona have all the answers, Olivia. I only know that magic doesna happen without purpose. And no part of me believes ye were meant to come here for a time and make us all care about ye, only to leave. I've said me piece. Ye must figure out the rest on yer own."

I could no longer concentrate on the baking project in front of me. As I glanced down at the wet, mushy mess, unable to recall how much of the last few ingredients I'd thrown in, I pushed it away as I cast irritated eyes in Miren's direction.

I'd wanted distraction, and instead Miren had driven me to face a truth I'd been much too scared to allow myself to admit—I was in love with Paton. And even if it meant being separated from my sister, I really didn't want to go home.

CHAPTER 35

Morton Castle

"I doona enjoy hurting ye, lad. But ye canna blame a father for doing what he must to assure vengeance for his son, can ye?"

Sweat soaked Davy's clothes, and he shook violently as the now broken fingers of his left hand racked with pain. If this continued, he would die.

Davy struggled to keep his wits about him as Laird Morton continued to drone on. He would have to proceed carefully. If he said too much, his death was inevitable. If Laird Morton learned that he'd crossed paths with the chef—that he knew the truth about Paton's so-called debts, the old laird wouldn't hesitate to put an end to his life.

Too little information would also unleash Laird Morton's

anger in a way he wouldn't escape. So, what was the answer? How could he create a believable lie?

"I'll ask ye again, lad. What did Paton send ye to do? Ye moved the lass, aye? Ye hid her away somewhere to protect her from the consequences of her actions."

"Nae." He spoke through parched lips and his throat ached from screaming. "I give ye me word, I dinna move the lass, but my task did involve ye."

"Oh?" Laird Morton lowered his mallet and sat in a chair across from the one where Davy was tied. "Have ye finally decided to tell me the truth then? If ye dinna leave the isle to hide the girl, then what did ye leave the isle to do?"

"He sent me to seek counsel. To see if ye could truly hold him to a debt acquired by his father."

Davy held his breath as Laird Morton stared at him. It was a believable enough story, but if Laird Morton could see through it, Davy knew he would have to brace for the end.

After a long pause, Laird Morton narrowed his eyes at him and spoke.

"And? What did ye learn during yer time away?"

"That ye can. When Paton inherited the land from his father, he inherited the man's debts, as well."

Davy allowed himself a breath as Laird Morton let loose a sly smile at his answer.

"O'course, I can."

Laird Morton stood and crossed the room to pour something into a glass before bringing it back to him.

"Drink, lad. Ye are in need of it."

Davy gulped down the lifesaving water as Laird Morton bent to whisper in his ear.

"Do ye see how easy this can be if ye only tell the truth? Now, where is the girl?"

He knew Laird Morton wouldn't accept his feigned ignorance. If he wanted to live, he would have to tell Laird Morton the truth and hope against hope that Paton and his men were strong enough to best Laird Morton and his.

"The last time I saw her, she was inside the castle. That is all I know or can tell ye. Now ye must either kill me or let me go. I've naught else to give."

Laird Morton turned away from him long enough to address the burly man who stood guard in the corner of the room.

"Ready the men. We shall ride for Buchannan Castle at once. Paton has broken his word to me, and for that, he shall pay."

When he turned back toward Davy, fear gripped at his throat as he watched Laird Morton's eyes fill with glee.

"Ye've only listed two things that I may do with ye, but there is a third. I can always throw ye into the dungeon and let ye die a slow death there. And that, me poor, unlucky, lad is precisely what I shall do."

The guard crossed the room quickly then, yanking him up from the chair before dragging him across the room and casting him down a set of stairs and into darkness before he heard the latch lock behind him.

CHAPTER 36

Buchannan Castle

Each night he held her in his arms grew harder. Each time she reached for him as she slept, snuggling close for warmth, he wondered how he would possibly be able to let her go? How could he propose to any other when the only woman he would ever want already lay beside him?

Damn his bad luck, and his father's poor choices.

Davy would return home soon. While he knew it to be wrong, every bit of him hoped there was no longer a portal to be found that could send her home.

"Paton?"

"I thought ye were asleep, lass."

"No. Why aren't you sleeping?"

"Me mind is too full, and me heart too heavy."

Her lips found his in the darkness as she turned toward him. She kissed him softly, and then reached up to run her hand through his hair, scratching at his scalp in a way that instantly released some of the tension in his body.

"What's on your mind?"

Over their nights together they'd talked of much. Of her life and time, of her family and bakery. Of his past. The one thing they'd both avoided was any talk of each other—of them as a unit. But tonight, he could no longer hold all he felt for her inside.

"Of what else, but ye, lass. Ye have occupied me every thought since I met. I worry I shall go mad from it."

She pulled her hand away from his head and moved it flush against his chest.

"Paton, I know we don't know for sure that a way for me to get back home even exists. But even if it does, what if I didn't go?"

His breath caught in his throat at her question. Was it possible the lass felt as deeply for him as he did for her?

"Do ye no longer wish to return to yer home? What of yer sister? Yer family?"

"I would miss all of them terribly, and if there was any way possible, I would want to give my sister the solace of knowing I'm well and happy where I am. But Paton, I'm afraid if I left here, I would miss you even more. I know this isn't fair to you. It's not convenient, but I've not stayed true to our agreement. I'm deeply, madly, obsessively in love with you."

He thought his heart would burst from happiness as he bent his head to kiss her.

"And I ye, lass."

She pulled away from him for the briefest of moments as she spoke against his lips.

"Say the actual words, Paton. I have dreamed of hearing them from you."

"I love ye, Olivia Bailey. None in me entire life have filled me heart with as much joy as ye have these past days. I know we havna known each other long, but I know me heart well enough, and in yer hands it finally feels at home. But, lass, I fear I must still marry another."

My emotions shifted quickly as Paton spoke to me. Hearing him say he loved me filled me with joy, but it was a feeling quickly muted by his admission that our love for one another changed nothing in terms of what he felt obligated to do.

I'd spent the rest of the day following my conversation with Miren racking my brain for an answer, but nothing had come to mind until I lay sleeplessly in bed with Paton. The idea wasn't fully fleshed out, but I could see no better time than now to mention it to him. At this point, anything was worth a shot.

"What if you didn't have to marry someone else? I have an idea."

"I am open to anything that might save me from any fate that would separate me from ye, lass."

I braced myself for his inevitable rejection of my plan as I began.

"What if instead of acquiring the money through marriage, you just sought a clan that could loan you the money for a short period of time? Foster good relations with the next laird that arrives, try to make friends, and explain your situation and see if they would take on the debt for you in exchange for you paying them back more than you currently owe Laird Morton."

Even in the dark, I could sense his hesitant expression.

"But lass, while such a plan might release me from being bound to Laird Morton, 'twould only bind me to another. I would still have no way to pay back the debt, no matter where the money is owed."

His argument was unsound. Nothing was as binding as a marriage.

"And you think a marriage won't do that? And yes, I know that you don't have the means to repay your debt, but I think I just might."

He laughed, and I tried to brush off the insult I felt at him not being able to wrap his head around an unmarried woman with money.

"I doona remember seeing satchels full of coins tied around yer waist when ye arrived here."

"I didn't say I had the money here. But if we can find a way back to my own time, I think I could pull together the money you would need to repay your new debt. Rory and I sold our bakery before we left on this trip, and half of the proceeds belong to me. We made a lot. The value of things now is much greater in my time, so I expect what I have from the sale will be enough. Gold would surely be accepted as payment, right?

"Aye, lass. There is none that wouldna accept gold."

"I could use everything I have to buy as many gold bars as possible. And then we could come back. Right now, you could find a clan willing to pay the debt for you, and then once things with Laird Morton have calmed down and it's safer to try to take me off the isle, we could go to my own time to get my money. It would also give me the opportunity to find Rory and tell her about my decision to stay here."

I didn't breathe as I waited for him to answer. When he finally did, his voice was low and soft.

"'Tis no' the worst idea I've ever heard."

"Is it enough of an idea for you to not propose to the next girl that shows up at the castle tomorrow?"

"Aye, lass. It is that."

I exhaled and scooted back down in the bed.

"Good. I think we can make it work, Paton. If there's a way for me to get here, there has to be a way to get me back. Even if Davy doesn't find it, once things have settled, we can go in search of it ourselves. I love you."

"I love ye too, lass.

That's all I needed to know for tonight. I could rest easier knowing that the immediate threat of me losing him to another for the sake of this castle was on pause, at least for now.

CHAPTER 37

A stern knock on his bedchamber door stirred him from the most restful sleep he'd had in days. Worry filled him as he sat up in the darkness. Daylight was hours away. Who would be needing him at this hour?

Slipping beneath the covers, he reached for his kilt to cover himself as he stumbled along to the knock which only increased in volume as time went on.

He opened the door to see Chambers standing in the hallway, a candle in hand, and concern etched all over his face.

"What is it?"

"There is a caravan of people making their way up the castle path. Our guests were no' set to arrive until tomorrow, aye?"

Paton frowned. Why would anyone travel at nighttime?

"Aye. Do they carry the tartan of Clan Brighton?"

"Nae."

"Is it Laird Morton?"

"Nae, 'tis too many travelers to be Laird Morton."

Would he wake shortly? Could all of this be some sort of strange dream? If not their guests arriving early or Laird Morton coming to make trouble, who else with so many people would be arriving at the castle in the middle of the night?"

"I will be down straight away. Wake Bram and tell him to join me. The rest of ye stay inside until we call for ye. If there is trouble, we doona all need to be exposed at once."

Chambers gave him a nod and hurried down the hall in the direction of Bram's room.

He dressed quickly, taking care to lock Olivia inside as he left. If whoever approached meant them harm, at least there would be some barrier between Olivia and the mob that rode ever nearer.

He stopped long enough to light a torch from the fire that burned around the clock in the sitting room before stepping out into the freezing night air and situated it in its stand to light the entryway to the castle.

The horses were many, but the faces of those riding were still draped in darkness. Instead, he broadened his shoulders and called out toward his unexpected guests.

"Who is there? Please make yer name and yer intentions known at once, or I shall call for the guards."

"Paton? Oh my God, Paton, I am going to fucking kill you!"

His knees nearly gave out on him as the familiar voice pierced its way through the darkness. It couldn't be, but God how he hoped it was true.

He opened his mouth to call out again, to demand an answer to his question, but before he could do so, he heard feet drop onto the ground before he looked up to see a figure running toward him with impressive speed.

He barely had time to open his arms to her as Kate threw

herself against him and they both tumbled backwards onto the castle steps.

She sobbed against him as he pushed them both up from the ground, his breath ragged and pained as shock and disbelief shot through him.

"Kate?"

He pushed himself away from her in his haste to see her face, and to look to ensure that the lass standing before him was missing one arm. Years apart hadn't distorted his memory of her. There was no doubting it. Somehow, someway, Kate was alive.

"Yes, it is Kate! How could you do this to us, Paton? Do you have any idea how much I've worried about you every damn day since you took my place with those horrid creatures? How could you just leave the isle without a word to any of us? Did they turn you into one of them? Did they make you as cold and unfeeling as they are?"

Tears filled his eyes as he dropped to his knees and wrapped his arms around Kate's waist. She stopped screaming at him the moment he pulled her close. Instead, she lowered herself and wrapped her arm around him in another, more gentle, embrace.

"I thought ye were dead, lass. How are ye no' dead?"

"What do you mean? Of course, I'm not dead. Paton. Are you…are you okay?"

He continued to hold her tight against him as he sobbed.

"What of the others, lass? How many of them survived?"

"Paton…" It was Kate's turn to push him away, as she placed her palm on his cheek and brushed at his tears with her thumb. "Why do you think anyone is dead?"

Through chest racking sobs, he told her what he had seen

the day the faeries released him, and with each passing word, he watched her face grow hot with rage.

"Paton, they lied to you. They made you see things that weren't there. Everyone is alive. Everyone is well. And everyone is right here, ready to squeeze your neck right now."

"Aye, we are, lad. Now will ye release me wife from yer grip so the rest of us may have our turn with ye?"

Paton feared he might lose consciousness from the way his heart hammered inside his chest as he looked up to see those he'd long thought gone dismount their horses and walk toward them.

Tears continued to fall freely down his face as Maddock, Adwen, Nicol, and the others gathered him in a group embrace under the moonlit sky.

With Olivia's pronouncement of her love for him, and now the return of beloved friends, Paton felt the broken pieces of his soul begin to heal.

Maybe there could be more to his life than pain and disappointment.

Maybe things would turn out alright in the end.

CHAPTER 38

The brush of Paton's lips against my brow stirred me from my slumber, and as I opened my eyes to a room awash in sunlight, I knew I'd slept far past morning.

"I thought I would let ye sleep, lass, but I ne'er thought ye would sleep so long. I canna wait another moment to tell ye what has happened."

I smiled as he kissed my cheek, and I thought I could hear the sound of laughter from somewhere down below.

Paton's eyes were bright, the line between his brow smoother than I'd ever seen it. He looked different—happy, glowing, at peace.

I pushed myself up in the bed. "What is it?"

"They're no' dead, lass. None of them."

It took my just-awakened brain a few seconds to compute. "Who isn't dead?"

"All on the Isle of Eight Lairds, lass. They are well, and they are gathered in the dining hall this verra instant. I canna wait for ye to meet them. Will ye dress and join us downstairs?"

"Oh, Paton!" I threw my arms around him as joy for him shot through me, pushing away any remaining sleepiness. "How…how is that possible?"

"The fae are a meddlesome lot, lass, and they are capable of great harm. They tricked me, and I am ashamed that I was fool enough no' to see it. Though in truth, the possibility did cross me mind when ye told me of yer dream and interactions with Morna, but I couldna allow meself to hope for something that might not be true."

I pulled myself away from him and hurried to slip out of my nightgown. I was eager to meet all of them, as well. It would be great to see women from my own time, and perhaps seeing how they'd adapted over the course of many years here would give me even more confidence that I could do the same.

"What of the other clan that is due to arrive today?"

Paton sighed. "Aye, 'tis too late to stop them from coming. The journey is too long to have them turn around. I have Chambers watching for them as Clara and Miren hurry to ready rooms. Everyone shall have to share, 'tis the only way we shall have enough rooms. Still lass, mayhap if ye hurry, ye will have time to meet everyone before the others arrive and ye have to hide away again."

"Okay, I'll be down as quickly as I can. You go ahead. I know you need as much time with them as you can get."

He shot me a smile and hurried from the room and as I reached for the dress closest to me and donned it as quickly as I could.

The warmth and love in the dining hall as I entered was palpable. And it didn't take long before I was swept up into so many hugs and introductions that I knew it would take a miracle for me to remember everyone's names.

Those from the Isle of Eight lairds were a happy lot, and it did my heart good to sit back and watch as Paton interacted with them. For a long while, I sat silently amongst them, enjoying the opportunity to simply take everything in. But as the hours ticked by and the arrival of the new clan edged ever closer, I could sense Paton's mood dip ever so slightly.

Eventually, he leaned over in his chair and whispered in my ear.

"I think 'tis time for me to fill them in on what occurred between ye and Lanrick Morton. I must explain to them why ye canna be seen once Clan Brighton arrives."

I squeezed his hand to give him a little moral support before he turned to address the group.

"I canna tell all of ye how pleased I am to see ye here once again. With Laird Brighton and his family due to arrive, I fear I must tell ye of some misfortune that has caused some conflict on the isle."

I sat there watching everyone's expressions as Paton explained to them what I'd done, and why, and what that meant for me while the Brighton's were here for their visit. To my relief, all I could sense in the expressions of most at the table was support. The only one whose expression remained guarded was the older man, Nicol.

He stood from his seat to speak as Paton finished.

"Forgive me, Paton, but I doona believe ye've told us

precisely why ye've invited Laird Brighton to yer territory. Do ye know him?"

Now that our plans had changed regarding Paton's plan to propose marriage, I wondered how he would answer. With all of the catching up I knew they had to do, I doubted he'd yet explained anything to them about his father's unpaid debt to Laird Morton.

Before Paton could answer, Bram spoke up from across the table.

"My brother has decided it is time for him to marry. He hopes to make an alliance of marriage between our clan and Clan Brighton."

Immediately, all eyes in the room turned toward me and Paton. Everything from the way he sat near me to how he'd introduced me had made it plain for everyone to see that we were an item.

Still standing, Nicol pressed on.

"Truly, Paton? I canna imagine that this fine lass here is too thrilled with the idea. Nor yerself."

Paton shot his brother a frigid glance before answering.

"'Tis true that was my original intention. My plans have now changed, as me heart will no longer allow me to do as I planned, but 'twas too late to rescind my invitation."

"Why was that ever yer intention, lad? I have never known ye to be a fool. Only a fool would marry for anything other than love."

It was easy to see how Nicol could lead a group of men. Even though that was no longer his role within the group, they all seemed to accept his lead by default. Even Paton seemed younger and less sure in front of him.

Paton sighed, and I knew he had to be hesitant to air his

father's dirty laundry in front of so many he cared about. Even if we are each acutely aware of our own parents' flaws, that doesn't mean we want others to think of them as anything other than perfect.

"I suppose there is no harm in telling ye the truth of it. Ye are family. Each and every one of ye. Weeks ago, we were approached by the same Laird Morton who seeks to find Olivia for the murder of his son, with news about a debt our father owed him before his death. He had an agreement signed by our father's signet as proof of what was owed to him. I've no way to pay the debt. Me intention was to find a laird who would marry his daughter to me, and I would use the alliance to acquire the funds necessary to pay me father's debts."

Nicol, still standing, crossed his arms.

"Lad, do ye think it possible there was ever a time when yer father would've required three times the funds Laird Morton says ye owe him?"

"I canna imagine what circumstance in me father's life that would've required such a great deal of money, but as ye know, I wasna here for the years in which all of this took place. Though Bram can attest to the fact that there was a time when our father grew rather desperate for funds."

"Aye, lad. I am well aware of that. Do ye think it possible that others throughout Scotland did as well? Namely, Laird Morton?"

Paton looked over to address his brother.

"Bram ye were here, then. Were Da's troubles well known?"

Bram nodded. "Aye."

Nicol nodded. "I suspected as much. The reason I ask, lad, is because yer father wrote to me of these troubles a good many years ago, and I sent him the entirety of the amount he asked for, plus some. And all that I sent was not a loan, but a gift. I robbed yer father of a son, the least I could do was offer him aid when 'twas needed."

As I looked up to see the muscles in Paton's jaw clench tightly together, I knew our minds were landing on the same possible conclusion.

Perhaps the fae weren't the only ones to dupe him.

CHAPTER 39

Morton Castle

At least now that Laird Morton was readying his troops for an attempted takeover of Buchannan Castle, he and his men were too busy to torture Davy. The silence allowed him time to think, to make a plan, and to lure the dolt lone guard who stood outside his cell nearer him.

Laird Morton—the old fool—hadn't removed his dirk before throwing him into the dungeon.

While his left hand remained useless, his right would be enough to fell the man. Deciding he had to act if he had any chance of escaping in time to warn Paton, Davy stood and walked up the stairs to the cell door and spoke to the man standing one step too far away.

"Will ye do me a kindness, man? Tell me what the chances are that I make it out of here alive, and doona mince yer words. If I am to die in this cell, doona I at least deserve a chance to make peace with such a fate?"

The guard looked over at him, and to his surprise, he thought he could see a hint of empathy in the man's expression. It gave him hope that his ruse might work.

"Ye will die, lad. I have ne'er seen Morton release a man once placed in that cell."

He nodded, feigning resignation, as he sent up a silent prayer that the guard would take his bait.

"I've always had a weakness for ale, sir. I've no family to speak of, no love who shall miss me. 'Tis the ale I shall miss. Could ye find it in yer heart to spare me but a sip?"

The guard grumbled and then threw his arms up in exasperation.

"Why no', lad? Laird Morton is no' here to see it now, anyway."

Davy reached for the dirk in his boot as the guard turned his back toward him to pour him a drink. He hated the thought of killing a man, but if this man's death prevented that of those he loved, he would learn to live with himself.

With the blade hidden behind his back, Davy waited until the man's hand slipped through the bars to give him the cup. He moved quickly, jabbing the knife into the man's chest with his right hand before throwing the blade aside to catch the man's keys as he dropped to the ground.

Frantically, he fumbled with the lock as he listened to the man gurgle and die. Once he was free, he fled into the darkness. With any luck he would make it to Buchannan Castle by sunrise.

Buchannan Castle

Tables had to be brought in from the sitting room to accommodate everyone at breakfast the next morning, and both brothers joined Miren in the kitchen to help prepare the feast for the crowd.

"What did Laird Brighton say when he arrived and saw that the castle was already brimming with guests?"

Miren continued to load his arms with trays as Paton stood as still as he could to keep from dropping them onto the floor.

"He handled it better than I woulda. He seemed excited to meet even more people that he dinna know. Is everything ready? I doona think I can carry anything else. And ye will run a meal up to Olivia as soon as we set these down, aye?"

Miren nodded and waved him from the kitchen.

"O'course I will. Aye, all is ready. Though I have ne'er cooked for so many before. I hope everything is edible."

He had no doubt that it would be.

Together, the three of them spread the feast around the room. Once all began to eat, Paton settled himself at the end of the table.

Just as he began to raise the first bite of food to his mouth, he could hear the doors to the castle burst open. It took only seconds for Davy to come crashing into the dining hall as he gripped the doorway and fought for his breath.

Alarmed by the bloodied and dirty sight of him, Paton stood and rushed over to his side.

"Davy, what has happened to ye? Were ye attacked?"

Davy stood, placed his hand on his chest, and continued to breathe fast and hard.

"I ran all night, Paton. I am sorry to appear before yer company in such a state, but this canna wait. I just escaped from Laird Morton's dungeons. The man is a filthy bastard, Paton. 'Tis a lie Paton, all of it.

"I stopped at a village on the mainland on me way to Cagair Castle, and Gawen was there, Paton. He told me the reason he left here. Laird Morton forced him to steal yer father's ring. And Gawen fled with his family to keep Laird Morton from killing them. The document he showed ye was forged. Yer father ne'er owed him anything."

Paton moved to wrap Davy's arm over his shoulders as he called out to Clara and Chambers for assistance.

While Davy's news came as no real surprise after Nicol's admission, it would serve as the confirmation he needed to end all this straight away.

"Good God, lad, I owe ye a great deal."

Davy stepped away from him, staggering as he gripped the doorway once again.

"There is more, still. I told Laird Morton that Olivia was here. 'Twas the only way I could keep him from killing me. He and his men march for the castle as we speak. While I was able to pass them, they are edging ever closer. At the pace they move now, they will be here by sunset."

Paton thanked Davy once more as Chambers led his friend from the room. Turning toward the shocked faces of Clan Brighton and the battle-ready ones of those already clued in on what was happening, Paton knew they would all have to come together as one if they were to survive the day without casualties.

CHAPTER 40

"No." I stood firm in the doorway blocking Paton as he moved to leave.

"Lass, we have no choice. There are women and children here. We canna permit Laird Morton to get onto the castle grounds."

"Will you just shut up for a second and listen to me?" My tone was harsher than I'd intended, but I was just as aware as he was of the fact that we were quickly running out of time, and I wasn't about to allow a whole group of men to go into battle over something I'd done.

Paton must've seen the desperation in my expression, for he stilled long enough to give me one solemn nod.

"Fine, lass. What is it ye wish to say?"

"I know very well that you can't allow Laird Morton to get onto the castle grounds. My experience with his son was enough to clue me in on what the man is capable of. But he's not coming here because of the fake debt he's trying to extract from you, Paton. He's coming here for me. Every man you intend to bring with you has people who love them. Some of them have wives and children. I won't allow them to risk their lives for me. There must be another way."

He shook his head as he placed his hands on my arms and tried to move me, once again, out of his way. I pressed my back hard into the door to try to slow him.

"I am sorry, lass, but there is no other option. We must ride at once. I love ye, and I shall return to ye, but ye must get out of me way."

"Yes, there is. It's an obvious one. And I know you've already thought of it."

He tightened his grip on my arms as he glared down at me, his jaw tight and angry once more.

"I am no' giving ye to him, lass. I'd rather see every man here dead than witness what Morton would do to ye if he got his hands on ye. I've lost them once before. I can survive it again. But I…" his voice broke as he buried his face into my neck. "I couldna survive losing ye, Liv."

His lips sought mine, and the desperation in his kiss told me all I needed to know. Even if he would never admit it, he knew my suggestion was the only way forward.

"Paton." I pulled away from him. "I'm not suggesting you let me die, but you know as well as I do that the best way to end this is to let him have me. Or at least permit him to think that you are doing so. Thayne needs to die, but that means you will need to lead his territory once he is gone. If there's a battle in which men from his territory die, it may be difficult to oversee people who only see you as a brute. If we can end this with only Thayne's death, I'm certain the men would prefer you as their laird."

Paton growled as he began to pace and rage his way around the room.

"How do we keep him from killing ye straight away, lass?"

"We have to come up with a way for me to kill him first."

"If ye kill Laird Morton, lass, his men will kill ye right away."

"Your men will be there, and hopefully their presence will cause Morton's men to think twice about killing me. I know it's no guarantee, but it's a gamble we have to take. There's simply no other way around it."

"I doona wish ye to go, Bram. Please. I am begging ye. If both ye and Paton should die, who shall oversee this territory? Who will keep me safe from Murray once he recovers? I only just found ye, Bram. I canna lose ye now."

Miren clung to Bram's kilt with a desperation she'd never felt in her life. And while she knew her pleas would fall on deaf ears, it was all she could do as she watched the man she loved prepare to ride out with the others.

"I willna die, lass."

"Ye canna know that for sure."

"Aye, Miren, I do. Had I faced Morton's men a fortnight ago, I might have hoped for death. But now I've someone to return home to. I promise ye, lass, I shall return to ye. And when I do, I want ye to become me wife."

Miren's face flushed red with anger at Bram's false promise.

"Ye know 'tis no' possible, Bram. I am still married. None on this isle will e'er see us wed."

He grabbed her then, lifting her deftly into his arms as he

kissed her and spun her so that he could lay her back on the bed.

"I've been wanting to tell ye all day, lass, but this is the first time I've had ye alone. A messenger arrived from the village amidst all the chaos this morning. Ye are no longer married. Ye are widowed. And widows may wed any time they wish."

Miren could scarcely believe it.

"How? When? Please tell me that ye dinna kill him, Bram."

"Lass," he lowered himself on top of her as he trailed kisses along her chin. "The last time I laid eyes on Murray Black was the same time ye did. He died in his sleep. They think 'twas his heart."

How a heart could keep on beating inside a man as evil as Murray Black for as long as it did, Miren would never understand.

"If ye doona return to me, Bram, I shan't forgive ye for it."

"Aye, lass. I know. I shan't forgive meself, either."

CHAPTER 41

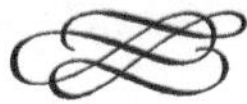

Davy stared at me blankly as Paton told him our plan. When he finished, he simply shook his head.

"She shall end up dead. She hardly looks strong enough to knock a man over, let alone stab a man in the heart."

To his credit and to my surprise, Paton didn't back down from our plan at Davy's warning. Instead, he pulled the blade from his kilt and extended it in his friend's direction.

"She can do it. She has no other choice. Please, Davy, just show the lass precisely where the blade must enter him to kill Laird Morton as quickly as possible."

Davy stood, his appearance slightly improved thanks to Clara and Chamber's efforts to clean him up and see to his hand.

"And why am I the one ye have asked to show her this?"

"Did ye no' just tell me that ye escaped a dungeon by killing a man in much the same way? Yer past is far more sordid than mine, Davy. Will ye help us or no'?"

Reluctantly, Davy took the blade from Paton's hand and hesitantly pressed his fingertip to its tip. A drop of blood instantly appeared on his skin.

"At least ye've given her a sharp blade. 'Twill help. And aye, I will show the lass what to do, as long as ye give me your word that ye willna hold me responsible if all of this goes poorly."

"I swear to ye, lad. I know what ye have already done for us."

Assured that the blame would be solely my own if I was to perish, Davy proceeded to show me where to hide the blade in my dress, how to reach for it with the right hand, and precisely where to drive it into Laird Morton's heart.

Had someone told me a month ago that in the span of a few weeks, I would've already killed one man and would be readying myself to kill another, I never would've believed them.

But I was now in a very different time, with very different rules. And despite my strong opinions on taking someone's life, I knew that one thing was crystal clear now—Laird Morton's death was the only way this would ever end for any of us.

Never in his life had Paton been gripped by such ardent fear. Every part of him ached to turn his horse around and take Olivia back to the castle, throw her in his room, lock the door, and throw away the key.

But he knew he could not. Lanrick Morton was responsible for this, not she, but no matter how he tried to convince her otherwise, Paton knew that Olivia saw this as her fight. If he denied her the ability to make her own decisions, she would never forgive him. And that was no way to begin their life together.

"Where are they?"

He spoke over his shoulder toward Bram, but his brother didn't seem to hear him. As he looked in the direction in which Bram now stared, he could see precisely where'd they gone. Toward the cliff at the end of the road which separated their two territories—to the clearing where a battle could easily be fought. It was just about the only place on the entire isle where the ground was flat and there would be nowhere for any man to hide.

Pushing away his desire to run, Paton instead urged his horse to run faster, and it didn't take long for Laird Morton and his men to come into view.

"He must've had a man stationed near the castle. Someone has warned him that we learned he was on the move. Rather than continue their march to the castle, they've stayed here and awaited us to come to them. Doona dismount until I've said everything that we planned, aye, lass?"

He whispered the words into her ear as they neared the point where he would no longer be able to speak to her without alerting Laird Morton to the nature of their relationship.

"I won't."

"I love ye, lass. Doona hesitate when the time comes to stab him. Move quickly, confidently, and end this for all of us. I know ye can do this."

"I know I can, too. Now let's end this. Together."

He admired her confidence, and he hoped she couldn't see the way his hands shook as he held the reins in front of her.

"Ye've brought her with ye. I am pleased to see it, Laird Buchannan. Have ye come to yer senses and decided to turn her over to me?"

Paton pulled his horse to a stop as his men, The Eight, and

Laird Brighton lined up behind him, matching the pattern of Laird Morton's men. They were evenly matched in numbers, but not in strength. If things went poorly, he and his men would destroy Laird Morton's entire force.

"Aye, I have. Though I will only do so if ye allow me to address yer men first."

Laird Morton squinted at him, and Paton could tell that the old man was trying to work out what Paton was playing at.

"All ye ask in exchange for the murderess bitch is to say a few words in front of me men? Aye, lad. Go ahead. I canna see the harm in it. They will see yer lies for what they are."

Paton dismounted before turning to help Olivia off the horse. Once both her feet were on the ground, he stepped in front of her, shielding her as he moved to address Thayne's men.

"I only wish for each of ye to know the truth about the lass Laird Morton intends to kill in front of ye here today. She dinna murder his son as he has led ye to believe. The lass was only defending herself from rape and killed Lanrick Morton by accident in her haste to get away from him.

"Ye should also know that yer laird is a liar. For weeks now he has threatened me and me family saying he would take Buchannan land if I dinna pay a debt he claims me late father owed to him. I've just found proof that no such debt ever existed.

"I've a feeling ye all know the sort of man who owns the land ye live and raise yer families on. But now that Lanrick is dead, he has no living heir, and Laird Morton canna live forever. When the day comes that he should die, 'tis me intention to combine Morton land with Buchannan so that ye can live with the same fair rents and wages that those in me territory always have. When the day comes, I give ye me word I shall care for ye far more than Morton ever has."

Laird Morton's men remained expressionless throughout his speech, and it only took seconds of silence for Laird Morton to begin to cackle in a laughter that sent chills all the way down his spine.

"How did ye find out, lad? I was so sure my ruse would work."

"Me man, Davy, discovered the truth, and it seems ye are as talentless at keeping prisoners as ye are at keeping yer offspring alive. He escaped from yer castle last night, Thayne, and arrived this morning to tell us the truth."

Laird Morton's eyes flashed with anger, but he kept his voice calm as he spoke.

"Hand the lass over to me, and this can all end, Paton. I willna advance me men. Ye doona advance yers. One lass for the lives of all these men. It seems a fair trade to me."

He nodded and reached behind him for Olivia's arm as he pulled her from behind his back and into view.

"I agree. But here are the rules, Thayne. Only ye and I shall meet in the middle. We shall both leave our swords on the ground, and I will hand her off to ye once we are away from all the others. Should any man on either side step out of line, both sides may attack."

Laird Morton smiled, and Paton had to swallow to resist the urge to scream at Olivia to run.

"Verra well, lad." Laird Morton unsheathed his sword and laid it on the ground behind him as Paton moved to do the same.

It was time.

CHAPTER 42

Everything happened much too quickly once Paton and Laird Morton reached the center of the road between each territory. Just as Paton released my arm, and Laird Morton grabbed onto me, I moved to reach for the knife. But it was too late. Laird Morton had already spotted it—he'd probably spotted it during my walk toward him—and in a flash he pulled it from my gown, twisted my arms behind me, and placed the blade against my throat.

"Och, Laird Buchannan, please tell me ye dinna know the lass carried this with her?"

I watched every last drop of color drain from Paton's face as his eyes locked with mine and my legs began to shake.

Thankfully, though, Laird Morton mistook Paton's expression. Rather than concern for me, he took it to be a sign of his innocence.

"Ne'er ye mind, lad. Ye needn't answer. I can tell by the way ye look as if ye might piss yerself that ye had naught to do with this wee bitch's plan to kill me. I shall no' set me men to charge, although I probably should. But I must demand one more thing of ye before we leave. Watch the lass die. If ye take one step to leave, we will descend into battle."

Paton couldn't seem to tear his eyes away from me, but somehow, he managed to answer, his voice cracked and broken.

"I shall stay where I am."

For the briefest of seconds, Laird Morton turned his back to Paton as he lowered the blade from my neck, tucked it into his kilt, and grabbed my wrist. With his eyes still locked on me, Paton began to reach for his sword, but I quickly shook my head no as I tried to warn him to stop. I knew it took everything inside him to listen to me, but before Laird Morton glanced back over his shoulder, Paton closed his eyes in resignation and stood back as if he'd never moved.

"What was it ye said to me the first day I saw ye, lass? That ye'd fallen all the way down a cliff and somehow survived it? What are the chances ye can do so twice?"

Turning toward the cliffside, Laird Morton began to drag me along behind him, and it seemed a sort of sick serendipity that all of this would end in much the same way it had started.

As I stumbled along behind him, my mind raced for what I could do. Just as we reached the edge and Thayne turned toward me, grabbing my shoulders in an effort to toss me over, I blurted out the only thing that came into my mind.

"You can't kill me."

He smiled at me, and I knew that most likely my last words on this earth would be a lie.

"Is that so, lass? For 'tis precisely what I intend to do."

"I'm carrying your heir."

I wasn't even sure the math added up. Even if Lanrick had

succeeded in raping and impregnating me, I didn't think enough time had passed for me to know about it. But I also knew that Laird Morton was unlikely to know that. I also suspected that the loss of his heir had truly been the most difficult part about losing his son.

As soon as the words escaped my mouth, I saw his expression twist into something that resembled both disbelief and hope. His tortured tone let me know I'd made the right gamble.

"It canna be, lass. Ye said me son tried to rape ye. No' that he succeeded."

"I lied. He did succeed, and that is why I killed him. But a part of him grows inside of me now. The only remnant of your son left on this earth."

My confidence grew as I watched Laird Morton wrestle with the possibility in his mind.

"How can I know that this is no' just another one of yer lies?"

I shrugged beneath his tight grip.

"You can't. But do you really want to risk it?"

His hands dropped from my arms, and I knew the only chance I had to save myself was here.

Just as I'd done with his son, I lifted my knee high and swung my foot toward the center of his chest with all the strength I could muster.

And as I watched Laird Morton tumble off the edge of the cliff, I knew that, unlike my first tumble into this time, there was no way in hell he was going to survive.

CHAPTER 43

Three Months Later

The months following Laird Morton's death were some of the happiest of my life. While Laird Brighton's clan left shortly following the altercation, everyone from the Isle of Eight Lairds stayed on as we enjoyed a full, happy, and chaotic time of communion with those Paton had missed so much.

Only one thing soured the joy I felt. Always at some point during each day, I would think of my sister, and a familiar guilt and longing would pull me out of the moment. Then all I could do for a while was think about how much I missed her.

Miren had made an important point the day she spoke so bluntly to me in the kitchen—she was right to say that Rory didn't need me—to help me see that we did deserve our own lives. But that didn't mean that I didn't want her in my life at all. For my entire life, she'd been my best friend. While I loved spending time with the other modern women from the isle, I longed for my sister.

I wanted to hug her and explain everything that had happened. To apologize for leaving her alone for so long.

A playful smack on my behind pulled me from my melancholy thoughts as Paton snuck up behind me and nibbled at my ear.

"Yer thinking of yer sister again?"

I nodded as his arms came around me and I leaned back into his chest.

"Yes. But I'm okay."

"Come with me, lass. I've a surprise for ye."

Taking my hand, he led me from the castle sitting room back up to our bedchamber and over to the window where we could see the road leading up to the castle.

"Do ye see the riders approaching, lass?"

I nodded. "I do, but do you really think we have room for any more guests?"

"I've a feeling ye shall wish to make space for this particular guest, lass. Look closely. Does the middle rider look familiar?"

Rory.

Stunned, I swung around to face him as I threw my arms around his neck and pulled him close.

"How? How did you do this?"

He laughed and pulled my arms loose.

"In truth, I had little to do with this. It seems yer sister has been under the witch, Morna's, care since ye arrived in this time. Gillian and Orick live at Cagair Castle in your own time where the portal is, and they sent word last week that they would be traveling through with yer sister and that they would escort her to the castle."

I planted a big, giant smooch on him before I ran from the room, down the castle steps, and out the front doors toward my sister. The moment we locked eyes, we both burst into tears.

"You're gonna have to hang on a second, Liv. I'm not sure I can get off this beast of a horse by myself."

"I'm just impressed you're on it at all."

A stunning beast of a man, who I could only assume was Orick, dismounted with ease before walking over to help my sister off her horse.

Once she was on the ground, we collided with such force that we both nearly fell to the ground.

"Oh Rory, I have missed you so much. I am so, so sorry. I have so much to tell you, so much to explain."

She stepped back and held out a hand to stop me.

"Actually, I don't think you do. I've spent the last month with this crazy, jolly, infuriatingly loveable witch named Morna, and I'm pretty sure there's not a bit of your journey she hasn't filled me in on."

"And you believe all of it? Like you don't think we've both lost our minds?"

"I am fully aware that I should think we've lost our minds, but somehow, I don't. I think the witch must've given me something early on to help me chill out and accept everything. Whatever she did, I'm cool with it."

"Are you staying?"

She hesitated, and my heart sank just a little. Of course, I couldn't expect her to move hundreds of years in the past just for me, but part of me hoped that she would.

"I'm not sure yet. All I know now is that there's something about to happen that I just knew I didn't want to miss."

"Lass?"

Paton's voice called to me from behind, but as I glanced over my shoulder he was nowhere to be found.

"I'm down here, lass. Perched uncomfortably on one knee in the dirt. I have been informed by lassies that know far more than me that this is what is expected, so here I am, Liv."

I smiled as my heart began to race in anticipation.

He held a small wooden box as he smiled widely at me, his dimple on full display as he opened it. I looked down at the prettiest little ring I'd ever seen.

Everything about it was absolutely perfect.

"I know that I doona deserve ye, lass, but I will forever be grateful to the meddling witch and the sheep who shoved ye right off the cliffside and into me heart. I promise ye that I will spend each moment of the rest of me life loving ye.

"My mother's ring held three stones, lass. I've had each one placed into three different rings. Bram has given Miren one, and Ella has placed another on a string around her neck. 'Twould be the honor of me life if ye would allow me to place this third ring on yer finger, lass. Will ye marry me, Liv? I want naught more in this world than for ye to be me wife."

"Of course, I will."

Paton slipped the ring on my finger. As he pushed himself up from the ground, he pulled me into his arms as all those gathered on the castle steps began to cheer.

CHAPTER 44

In a bit of irony I seemed to find stranger than anyone else at the castle, Paton had a very specific request as to where he wanted to get married—at the fairy pools here on the Isle of Skye. But he seemed to know precisely what he wanted, and after much insistence that the fae he'd been taken by wouldn't, in fact, be at these pools, I'd agreed.

Since everyone we cared about was already gathered at the castle, and not one but two engagements had happened in a matter of weeks, Bram, Miren, Paton, and I had all decided that the thing that made the most sense was for us to make it a double wedding.

That was fine with me. As long as Paton was at the end of the aisle, I didn't mind if a chorus line of couples lined up to say their vows next to us.

The journey out to the pools was a difficult one, but once we arrived, I understood immediately why he'd chosen the location.

It was stunning.

And frigid.

And just as Nicol pronounced us man and wife, followed in short succession by Bram and Miren, the sky opened up and soaked us all to the bone.

If my suspicion was correct, we would all have enough good luck to last us the rest of our lives.

It truly was the happiest day of my life.

Shortly after we all arrived back at the castle, dripping wet and near frozen to icicles, I pulled Rory into her bedchamber while Paton worked to turn his room into a sort of a honeymoon suite for the two of us.

I didn't want to go to sleep on the night of my wedding worried about how many days I had left before my sister decided to go home, not when I had news which would almost certainly convince her to stay.

"What are you doing, Olivia? Shouldn't you be with your husband right now?"

I smiled at her and waved a dismissive hand.

"I've got all night to be with him. I just needed to ask you something."

She cocked her head suspiciously at me. "What?"

"Do you think you could extend your trip for at least another seven to eight months?"

Her eyes widened, and her jaw dropped open. "No!"

I nodded. "Yes!"

"Well, of course I can! When are you due?"

"I'm not sure. Less than seven months for sure, but I need you to be here for a while after the baby comes."

Rory's eyes filled with tears. "Well, of course I will be here! Does Paton know?"

"Not yet."

"Well, I feel very honored. Yes. I will absolutely stay."

The day I thought couldn't possibly get any better just got a little bit brighter. I hugged my sister tight and headed across the hall to see the Daddy-to-be.

CHAPTER 45

That night, after we made love for the second time, Paton rose from the bed to get us both a glass of water. When he returned, he hesitated before climbing in beside me. I didn't miss how his eyes seemed to rake suspiciously over my body. It seemed the secret I'd been carrying for what felt like ages was finally giving itself away.

I smiled at him as he climbed in behind me.

"What? Why did you look at me like that?"

He tried to pass it off as nothing, but I knew I'd not mistaken the hope in his eyes.

"I dinna look at ye any way, lass. No more than I always do, I mean."

I rolled over to face him, my smile mischievous and teasing.

"Oh, don't do that. Don't act as if I'm crazy. I saw you. Why'd you look at my body like that?"

He hesitated, his brows furrowing uncomfortably. "I doona

think our wedding night is the right time for me to say anything that could be taken poorly if I am wrong, lass."

I smiled. "Just ask, Paton."

His face lit up as he moved his hand to my stomach. "So the bulge here is more than just Miren's cooking then?"

I leaned forward to kiss him. "Yes."

He pulled back, his eyes full of wonderment and excitement as he stared at me. "When?"

"By my math, it was soon after I got here. Maybe even our first time. I guess it's a good thing that we both failed miserably at our initial agreement, huh?"

"Aye, lass. I canna bear to think about what I would've missed had ye chosen to go back home."

"Are you happy?"

He pulled me close and kissed me once more. "More than I ever dreamed I could be. I canna wait to see the life we create together."

Neither could I.

MORNA'S LEGACY SERIES:

Love Beyond Time
Love Beyond Reason
A Conall Christmas - A Novella
Love Beyond Hope
Love Beyond Measure
In Due Time – A Novella
Love Beyond Compare
Love Beyond Dreams
Love Beyond Belief
A McMillan Christmas - A Novella
Love Beyond Reach
Morna's Magic & Mistletoe - A Novella
Love Beyond Words
Love Beyond Wanting
The Haunting of Castle Dune - A Novella
Love Beyond Destiny
Love Beyond Boundaries

The Curse of McMillan Castle - A Novella
Love Beyond Magic

Collections:

Morna's Legacy: Books 1, 2, 2.5, & 3

Morna's Legacy: Books 4, 4.5, & 5

Morna's Legacy: Books 6, 7, & 7.5

Morna's Legacy: Books 8, 8.5, & 9

Morna's Legacy: Books 10, 10.5 & 11

BONUS EPILOGUE - SUBSCRIBE TO MY NEWSLETTER

Today when you sign up for my mailing list, I will send you a link where you can read and exclusive BONUS EPILOGUE for *Love Beyond Time* for FREE!

When you sign up for my mailing list, you will be the first to know about new releases, pre-orders, sales, and more. You will also get sneak peeks into books that aren't out yet. Just click one of the links in the paragraphs above or go to http://eepurl.com/hxS1kX to sign up today. I can't wait to connect with you there.

ABOUT THE AUTHOR

BETHANY CLAIRE is a USA Today bestselling author of swoon-worthy, Scottish romance and time travel novels. Bethany loves to immerse her readers in worlds filled with lush landscapes, hunky Scots, lots of magic, and happy endings.

She has two ornery fur-babies, plays the piano every day, and loves Disney and yoga pants more than any twenty-something really should. She is most creative after a good night's sleep and the perfect cup of tea. When not writing, Bethany travels as much as she possibly can, and she never leaves home without a good book to keep her company.

If you want to read more about Bethany or if you're curious about when her next book will come out, please visit her website at: www.bethanyclaire.com, where you can sign up to receive email notifications about new releases.

Connect with Bethany on social media or visit her website for lots of book extras:

www.bethanyclaire.com

facebook.com/bethanyclaire
instagram.com/bclaireauthor
amazon.com/author/bethanyclaire
bookbub.com/authors/bethany-claire
pinterest.com/bclaireauthor

ACKNOWLEDGMENTS

For a writer, I have rather irresponsible writing habits. I seem to need the terrifying crunch of a perilously close deadline to be able to squeeze any ounce of creativity out of myself. This makes it hard on those that play such an integral part in the book process. I hope you all know that I appreciate you so much. To Rori Bumgarner, Karen Corboy, Elizabeth Halliday, and Johnetta Ivey - thank you.

www.ingramcontent.com/pod-product-compliance
Lightning Source LLC
Chambersburg PA
CBHW030425310726
48979CB00009B/1619/J
* 9 7 8 1 9 7 0 1 1 0 7 1 5 *